ALSO BY MAX ALLAN COLLINS

———

TO LIVE AND SPY IN BERLIN

John Sand Book Three

MAX ALLAN COLLINS

WITH

MATTHEW V. CLEMENS

WOLFPACK
PUBLISHING
— EST 2013 —

WOLFPACK PUBLISHING
— EST 2013 —

To Live and Spy in Berlin

Paperback Edition
Copyright © 2021 Max Allan Collins

Wolfpack Publishing
5130 S. Fort Apache Road, 215-380
Las Vegas, NV 89148

wolfpackpublishing.com

Paperback ISBN: 978-1-64734-799-4
eBook ISBN: 978-1-64734-798-7
LCCN: 2021940816

TO LIVE AND SPY IN BERLIN

*Advance against the enemy
and the bullet might miss you.
Retreat, evade, betray
and the bullet would never miss.*

Ian Fleming

In memory of
BRIAN VAN WINKLE
a brave soldier

ONE

THE MEIER MISSION
JUNE 1963

CHAPTER ONE
LAST CHANCE FOR GAS

The relentless Nevada sun beat down on Stacey Sand as she moved cautiously down a gauntlet of dead neon signs discarded by nearby Las Vegas. Her long auburn hair pulled back in a tight ponytail, the petite but shapely woman—five foot four, not long past her thirtieth birthday—wore a black business suit with a white silk blouse, attire suitable for a CEO. Which, despite her age, and her sex, is what she was—specifically of Boldt Energy, as her late father's company, Boldt Oil, was now known.

The difference in wardrobe today was the shoulder rig under her especially tailored smart jacket, in which a Walther P38, twin to husband John Sand's pistol, snugly nestled.

She moved on, glancing at the craggy mountains of deceased neon signs on her either side, the electric refuse of defunct hotels, casinos, restaurants, and bars. In the shadows of these tall metal and glass tombstones in this consumer-culture graveyard, she sent her green eyes searching for motion, seeking a target to take down, an enemy agent say, or an innocent bystander to avoid.

She saw nothing. No movement. The only sound distant tumbleweed and a faint wind rustling it.

Another careful step later, however, movement flashed in the neon-and-steel pile to her right. Ducking, rolling left, she yanked the Walther from its nesting place, came up on one knee, and fired into the shadows where popped into view a man in a rumpled suit with a gun in hand. Her bullet caught him in the forehead, the crack of gunfire rattling metal, and a splash of red decorated the shadows as the figure seemed to disappear back within.

Then a stirring ahead at right announced a second thuggish shooter, a Middle-European type, slipping into view to point his revolver directly at her, and—still holding her breath—she rotated in the opposite direction and fired, prone. This presumed enemy agent took a hit squarely in the chest and fell from view between piles of dead signage, leaving a splash of blood behind him to drip down metal like scarlet paint.

She rose to a crouch, taking no time to dust off the expensive black suit, splotched gray by the gravel pathway she'd hugged. As she edged ahead, two more furrow-faced thugs materialized, both at left, one from between piles, the other up top, a sniper; she fired twice and they fell from view leaving blood mist behind. A rustle to her right made her pivot, then spin, as she pulled a switchblade from her waistband, snicked it open and hurled it, burying it in the chest of another thug on the right, his drab ill-fitting suit wearing a bloody dab of color now.

Sweat beaded her brow, but she didn't bother to wipe it away. Her entire focus was making it to the end of the aisle alive—up ahead, maybe ten yards, a mere thirty more feet...sunlight.

That shouldn't be so hard, should it? Living that long?

Another step. Two. Three, then a movement to her left brought her pistol up, but she didn't fire—the face in the shadows of the indentation where the figure stood could belong to friend or foe, and she dared not be cavalier about dispensing deadly force. The blue windbreaker with the big gold lettering—GUILE—announced a friendly. Who withdrew.

Three more steps and perhaps the threat was over, but *no*—she was in a crossfire! One directly at her left, another at right, and she dropped again, fired left, rolled, fired right, and both gunmen fell back into the shadows from which they'd emerged.

On her feet again, she quickly exchanged her empty magazine for a fresh one from a jacket pocket, ejected the empty, slammed the new magazine into place, racked the slide to chamber a round. Three more steps got her to aisle's end where a tall, muscular man in a GUILE windbreaker stepped out.

"Overall, I'd rate you high," Ronald Kisor said, with a weary smile, jotting something on the sheet of his clipboard. "Kind of breaks my heart to rate you a 'fail'".

"Failed in what respect?" she asked, keeping defensiveness out of her tone.

The Hogan's Alley here at the rural training center for GUILE agents had been challenging, but she knew she'd done well.

"Agent Kisor, all due respect—I took out every single enemy agent you threw at me. And there wasn't a civilian in sight."

Kisor, his blond flattop and blue eyes making a friendly if Master Race presence out of him, towered over her as he led her back up the aisle, slapping the clipboard off his leg as he walked. They passed the realistic manikins with movie-magic blood squibs making the gauntlet feel and look more real to the prospective agents. He stopped right in front of the agent in the GUILE windbreaker. She looked up at the manikin with its photographic face and Raven Nocona stared back at her...

...the notorious if very dead associate of the late Jake Lonestarr, the Texas-bred international criminal who had been responsible for her father's death.

"If you don't recognize *that* gent," Kisor said, faintly mocking, "I don't know what it would take. Adolf Hitler, maybe?"

"Damnit. Does this wash me out?"

"We'll discuss that, Candidate Sand. But for now, let's say this is as good a time as any for you to learn that not everybody dressing like a good guy is necessarily on the side of the angels."

"Noted," she muttered.

"Come with me."

She took the time to retrieve her switchblade from a dead manikin and followed Kisor back down the aisle to the massive, apparently ancient barn, its red paint all but stripped away, and around front to the sizeable Quonset hut connected to it. She trailed him up wooden steps to a porch and into what had been—her husband had told her—the antiques shop facade of the ultra-modern GUILE HQ within a barn that wasn't a barn at all.

GUILE, the Global Unit for Intelligence and Law Enforcement, was the secret organization with which her ex-MI6 agent husband was now affiliated; her training over, she would be a part of that too, unless she really had washed out due to her single Hogan's Alley flub.

Originally spearheaded by President John F. Kennedy, GUILE gathered agents from scores of member nations, with oversight provided by her husband's former supervisor Lord Malcolm Marbury, known informally as Double M by insiders. GUILE was tasked with handling the variety of world-threatening problems that paid no heed to borders, minus the usual bickering and treachery common among national intelligence services.

What had been the front business—a Vegas-themed antiques shop—was now a row of offices to one side and a classroom on the other. No academic testing was underway at the moment, but in the "barn" beyond was a massive training facility where she had spent much time over the past month, engaged in case exercises, firearms training, operational skills, and martial arts.

In Kisor's office, Stacey settled in the chair across from him as he worked at lighting up a pipe. The office was modest of size and as anonymous as the rest of the facility, although as this was the American wing of GUILE, an official color portrait of President Kennedy rode the wall; no stars and stripes in evidence, though, a nod to the international nature of the Global Unit.

"It's not my call," Kisor said, "but I don't have to tell you your husband's old boss demands perfection. You've excelled in every aspect of your training, in particular martial arts, although your instructor says you have your own ideas and methods on that score. Did Agent Sand train you in that respect?"

"No. My nanny did."

That raised almost invisible blond eyebrows as he waved out his match. "What sort of nursery was that, Candidate Sand? One just behind the Alamo?"

She smiled. "My chauffeur-cum-bodyguard, still in my employ but holding down the fort in Houston, is an ex-*federale*. Cuchillo—that's his name and preferred weapon—helped raise me."

"Well, even considering who your husband is," Kisor said, tapping the clipboard, "I can't look the other way. You failed the Hogan's Alley test at a key moment. That means you'll likely have to start over."

She sighed. "Not good news. I've been away from my business responsibilities too long already."

And she'd hoped for an actual field assignment with John, in which case being away from Boldt Energy was a sacrifice worth making.

Kisor shrugged, let some fragrant smoke out. "It will be up to Lord Marbury whether starting over is required. And up to *you*, whether you'll put yourself through this again—but, honestly, Mrs. Sand, I'm sure you'll breeze right through."

"Thank you."

After going over some of her other test scores, Kisor walked the candidate out of the office into the classroom area. "You must be anxious to get back to Houston," he said. "Or are you going to do Vegas up a little before you head home?"

"That hasn't been decided. The only thing I know for sure is we'll be making our usual stopover at the Moapa Diner. My husband's developed a taste for their 'Trademark Fried Chicken,' as the menu puts it. And it's the 'special,' served only on Friday."

Today.

Kisor chuckled around the pipe stem. "Back to the Moapa again, huh? Well, it *is* good, uh, chow. Still, fried chicken doesn't sound much like the kind of fine dining *Life* magazine reported...when they exposed John Sand as the real-life basis of a certain famous spy?"

She managed a smile, despite the disappointment she

hadn't yet shaken. "No. He *does* like his martinis, but whether they're shaken or stirred matters not a whit."

When Kisor escorted Stacey to the little wooden porch beyond which was parking for the instructors and candidates, her husband's MG convertible was already waiting toward the front. So was he, leaning against the sportscar, its British racing green paint job buffed to a high sheen; he was smoking a cigarette, no doubt one of those foul *Gauloises* numbers, which smelled to her more like burnt-rubber than peeling out in the MG.

Still, a woman could tolerate a lot worse from a man like this—tall, tan, dark-haired, with a face that knew it was handsome but didn't give a damn, the deep blue eyes concealed behind Ray-Bans, an athletic build that seemed designed for casual attire like the lightweight but tailored Madras blue-and-yellow jacket, the pastel blue Ban-Lon sports shirt, jeans and Italian loafers with no socks. The smile splitting his face upon seeing his wife made a liar of the *Life* writer who'd described such John Sand smiles as "cruel." He and Kisor exchanged little salutes and she went down to join this sophisticated man who was about to take her out for a mid-afternoon repast of fried chicken.

She fell into his arms and they kissed, lightly, before he said, "And how's my freshly minted GUILE agent?"

"She isn't one."

"Oh?"

He walked to her side of the car, opened its little half-door and she snugged inside, then looked up at him like he was a car hop ready to take her order. "I failed."

His frown was barely there, but it was a frown all right. He went around, got in and behind the wheel slipped the car into gear and was heading back toward the gate when he said, "Tell me."

She withdrew a scarf from the small glovebox, covered her hair as he waved at the guard who raised the gate arm, and as her husband turned out onto the back road, knotted the scarf under her chin and told him about the test.

"Not very sporting," he said, over the wind and the roar of the engine as they sped toward the interstate entrance ramp. "A shadowed face and a GUILE jacket."

She glanced over to see if he was being patronizing to her, but he seemed sincere enough—or was he just learning how to deal with a wife?

"I'm mad at myself, really," she said, as they headed away from the out-in-the-boondocks facility. "Apparent GUILE agent or not, he had a gun in hand. At the least I should have taken cover or a defensive position until I got a better look."

"I don't know this Kisor fellow well. Do you think he was trying to trick you?"

"Doubtful. But if I *could* be tricked, I *should* be tricked. The field gives no quarter."

"You're not wrong, darling," he said.

She squeezed John's hand on the gearshift and said, "So—how was your day? Fail to shoot any villains? Accidentally rack up any collateral damage?"

He gave her a little shrug, kicking the MG into fourth and speeding onto the four-lane highway. They were only going a few miles to the next exit, so not much time for small talk.

Over the combined symphony of the whistling wind and the roaring engine, he said, "Double M wants to see us this evening, for some reason."

"About what?"

"He wasn't forthcoming in that regard. Being his usual, annoying, mysterious self."

"Do you think...? Nothing."

"What?"

"Might he have been told I screwed the pooch?"

"Buggered the what?"

"Fouled up this afternoon."

Her husband shook his head. "This was earlier."

She shuddered. "He might not want to see us now."

They were flying along, but she felt safe. John could have raced at Le Mans, so skilled a driver was he. Anyway, she was no one to complain—they both loved speed, though she knew he could coax more out of the MG than she. He barely slowed as they veered onto the exit ramp, but by the stop sign, he had slowed.

With no traffic coming, they turned left, crossing the interstate to where the Moapa Diner sat waiting patiently— the last outpost of civilization before I-15 turned northeast toward Utah.

The two gas-pump islands at the Moapa Truck Stop and Diner—as denoted a neon worthy of the graveyard she'd just endured—weren't doing any business right now, though a semi was at the diesel pump alongside the building. The diner extended into a small motel where Bonnie and Clyde might have honeymooned. The few cars parked at the rear of the parking lot that faced the Moapa probably belonged to the staff of the gas station and diner. Otherwise, civilization seemed to have abandoned its last outpost. Maybe they hadn't heard about the trademark fried chicken.

John pulled the MG toward the front of the blacktop lot, turned off the ignition. Stacey untied her scarf, somewhat relieved the wind her husband had stirred up hadn't turned it into a noose, and he came around to open her door for her.

"Is my hair intact?" she asked him.

He helped her out. "It appears securely attached to your head."

"That's why I love you. Ever the romantic."

As he walked her toward the diner, he said, "Don't be greedy. You have a spouse whose looks don't scare small children, who is passable in bed, and is quite wealthy."

"You are wealthy by marriage," she reminded him, "and I *have* seen you scare small children."

"But you don't contradict the other?"

"No. You *are* passable in bed."

In the diner, the promised air conditioning seemed to be a technicality, barely cooler inside than out under the Nevada sun. A blonde waitress, pleasant, attractive, but with a good number of miles on her, hovered over by the pass-thru window to the kitchen, chatting with the cook in the back—otherwise the place was as empty as a politician's promise, which was no big surprise mid-afternoon.

"And us without a reservation," Stacey whispered.

"If they're out of fried chicken," he whispered back, "I will shoot up the place."

The diner could have accommodated at least three dozen customers, the U-shaped counter with a dozen and half stools to their left, and an L-shape of booths along the wall to the right and the far wall. The waitress turned toward them but didn't move. In a voice as matter of fact as a weather report, she said, "Anywhere you like, kids."

Stacey led him to the wall facing the counter, a trio of booths there, taking one in the middle between a cigarette machine and the bathrooms. A jukebox was playing country western, Rat Pack be damned. A row of slot machines off to one side had no takers.

The waitress came over, laid two menus in the middle

of the table like a dare and set two glasses of ice water down. Her name tag announced her as PENNY.

"Friday special is fried chicken with mashed potatoes and green beans."

That was always the Friday special. They had been here half a dozen Fridays, though this was their first chance to enjoy the personable Penny, who said, "Need a minute?"

John was about to order, but Stacey—who was not a fan of fried chicken, despite her Southern roots—said, "Yes, if you don't mind, please."

Penny gave them an it's-up-to-you shrug and walked away with her caboose barely keeping up.

Stacey's husband was frowning just a little—he'd apparently waited lunch for this—and his wife, gathering her clutch purse, assured him, "Gonna clean up a little—be right back."

"No rush," he said with a smile she almost believed.

She had the ladies' room to herself—just her, the smell of disinfectant, three stalls and a two-well sink. The mirror showed her a creature she considered horrifying—while John hadn't been lying about her hair...it was indeed still attached to her head...her face was grimy. As beauty treatments went, rolling around in gravel had proved among the least effective.

She huffed a sigh and got to work.

After a few minutes of beating the dust out of her jacket, washing her face and applying fresh lipstick and a few touches of make-up, she was ready.

When she stepped back into the dining area, what she saw stopped her—three apparent truckers were at the counter, and a touristy couple was in the booth behind her seat, another such couple in the booth behind John's.

How long had it taken her to reassemble herself,

anyway?

As she strolled back toward their booth, Stacey noticed that the truckers were clean-shaven with similar military-base style haircuts; terribly well-groomed truckers, and young ones at that—in their twenties, and with no long-haul flab. She'd noted the two tourist couples as painfully clean-cut in wardrobe right out of a Sears catalogue.

Something very phony was in the air.

Was this a field final for her GUILE training? An impromptu make-up test arranged by Kisor, who after all had known where she and John would be dining? And her husband had told her about his final test for MI6, when he had been confronted in a parking garage and had to defend himself against multiple attackers and yet make sure no innocent citizens were injured.

Much trickier than blood-squib manikins in a junkyard Hogan's Alley.

The couple behind Stacey included a thin blonde woman and a hulking male, older and brawnier than the young clean-cut truckers. When she passed by, the Hulk had been holding the oversized laminated menu in big hands that might have crushed it like a Kleenex.

Sliding in opposite John, she glanced at the booths beyond these three adjacent ones, over against the side wall under a Coca Cola clock. Two more men, both with military haircuts like the truckers at the counter, had settled in. Businessmen in off-the-rack suits. Sure.

She smiled uneasily. "Looks like we got here just in time."

"Doesn't it," he said, and there it was—the cruel smile. And a hard look in the blue eyes that said this was no drill, no final exam courtesy of Kisor. He glanced to his right, her left, to show her the direction she should move when the time came. They exchanged no other words, but he was speaking to her constantly with his eyes. His hands, flat on the table, said, *Stay calm.*

The blonde waitress returned, as if from a long journey. "Jeez Louise, I don't know where all these folks came from at once. We don't usually have a rush now. Better get your order in fast."

John smiled up at her. "Sorry to trouble you, but my wife left her purse in a stall in the bathroom."

Of course she hadn't. It was beside her in the booth, but out of sight between the seat and the wall.

John was saying, "Could you be a dear and go look for it?"

Penny shook her head and blonde hair flounced. "Look, mister, does it look like I have time to—"

John held up a hundred-dollar bill, just high enough for Penny to see. She took the bill and said, "Let me take a look right now, sir."

The waitress ducked into the recession where the restroom doors waited as Stacey watched John's eyes for the next signal. The sound of the bathroom door closing widened those eyes just a little and his right hand made a quick gesture toward Stacey's left. She quick ducked under the tabletop, crouching below as from the booth behind her a hand came arcing over, slamming a hunting knife into the back of the seat where a fraction of a second before Stacey had been. She peered over the tabletop—John was still in the booth, but on his feet, throwing ice water behind him in the face of a man now turned toward her husband, who smashed that glass, hard, into the tourist's face, enough to shatter. From under the Madras jacket came John's Walther while Stacey's gun emerged from her purse while John took out the three truckers at the counter—the reports were so fast they sounded like one long loud shot. They tumbled from stools to the floor spilling handguns they'd not got to fire. She looked up at her knife-wielding attacker, the big ugly tourist who yanked out that knife and was ready to climb over for another try when she shot him in the throat. He straightened, eyes wide, mouth wider, and was foaming blood when he toppled sideways to the floor. His thin blonde tourist "wife" opposite had a gun, some kind of semi-automatic, and Stacey shot her where forehead met bridge of the nose, those eyes widening too but their owner dying too quick for surprise to even register. The woman just sat there, a corpse ready to be waited on. Stacey scooted out from under the booth's tabletop and gave her attention to the booth behind John, whose male resident— shards of glass sticking out of his face and red teardrops coming from everywhere but his eyes, water beads from the glassful John had flung diluting the red—threw his arms around John from behind in a terrible hug; John still had the Walther in hand but his arms were pinned, so Stacey grabbed the gun from her husband's grasp and pressed the nose of the pistol to the tourist's water-soaked ear and squeezed off a round that sent a splattering stew of brain and blood against a picture of happy farmyard chickens on the wall. John grabbed the pistol back as the dead man slumped in the booth and Stacey's husband swung and shot the dead man's brunette "wife," who was screaming obscenities, her own gun in hand now, but she couldn't use it, not with a bullet hole in her forehead. Like the blonde "wife," she sat down and shut up.

The two businessmen in the booth across the room were heading for the door. John picked them off like ducks on the wing.

"Is that everybody?" she asked, looking around.

He nodded, helped her to her feet. "I'll check them."

This he did, quickly, and came back. "They're all dead."

"Good."

"Good and dead," he agreed.

The adrenaline was still flowing through her as they embraced. The whole gunfight had lasted less than a minute and nine potential killers lay waiting for their body bags.

That was when Penny came out of the bathroom. Where the woman had kept the .38 was a mystery, but she fired away with it, screaming.

As casually as if flicking a fly from his face, John took her out with a head shot that lifted her briefly before setting her on her ass and then on her back.

He gave Stacey a look. "Got to give her credit."

"For what?"

"She was a good actress."

"John!" Stacey blurted.

The cook, a heavy-set mustached man in white including apron, came out firing an UZI—its deafening churning thunder a terrible thing. Both husband and wife had already hit the deck when the cook began firing, and together Stacey and John Sand brought him down, the former with a body-mass shot, the latter through the head. Arguments would ensue over who deserved credit, but for now they again fell into each other's arms.

Then they got to their feet and brushed themselves off.

"As if rolling in gravel wasn't enough," she said, "I have to go crawling around under that table."

"You think *you've* got it bad."

"What?"

"No goddamned fried chicken," he said.

CHAPTER TWO

DESTINY

Outside the gleaming, cylindrical twenty-story hotel, in brightly colored lights, the huge sign flashed:

DESTINY
HOTEL & CASINO

While below neon letters spelled out:

WIN WITH US
IT'S YOUR DESTINY!

as green neon dollar signs danced on either side of the catchphrase.

Barely a year old, this shining citadel of a hotel attracted people from all over the globe, coming and going at all hours, making it the perfect cover for the new headquarters of GUILE, the fledgling organization moving into two upper floors shortly after an army of assassins invaded their former HQ at the neon graveyard. The effort to crush the multi-national Global Unit when it had barely been born was not about to dissuade the member countries from their goal of answering common threats from invasion-prone dictators, organized crime groups, and megalomaniac power-seekers.

Billionaire hotelier Donovan Drake, politically independent but a John F. Kennedy supporter—with anti-Cosa Nostra views in line with the President's Attorney General brother, Robert—welcomed GUILE as a major if unpublicized investor. The Global Unit would provide all the security for the hotel in exchange for rent-free space and a percentage of the casino/hotel's take, ensuring GUILE would be the only largely self-sustaining intelligence/law enforcement agency on the planet.

Drake was an ultra-reclusive millionaire who had made several fortunes as a gutsy entrepreneur. The rumor spread to the world at large that Drake and his entourage occupied the top three floors of the hotel, but in reality only the penthouse level was his. This kept most people from getting too curious about what went on up there. Drake was also rumored to have bodyguards who took his security seriously, as early on reporters had quickly learned after harrowing interrogation sessions with members of a formidable security force with an interestingly international flavor.

Normally, John and Stacey Sand—who for Mrs. Sand's month-long training period had been guests at the Destiny—would stroll in through the lobby toward the end of their day. Tonight, with a wardrobe whose blood spatter and dirt smudge might have been courtesy of Jackson Pollock—and after hours of questioning by the local constabulary before a representative of the Global Unit intervened—had opted for entry through a back door near the kitchen.

The Destiny's culinary and custodial staff, almost entirely GUILE support personnel, were used to encountering curious sights and circumstances disconcerting even for Las Vegas—blood-spattered, dirt-smudged agents, for instance.

Entering the service elevator, Sand pushed the button for seventeen, their floor. Soon they were locked within 1724, their three-room suite at the end of the hall, their home away from home but for the several days a week Sand commuted on Boldt Energy's Cessna 310 to oversee his wife's business interests—he was her executive vice president, after all. Stacey headed for the bathroom to clean up while Sand got out of his Madras sports jacket, which was even more colorful than before. When he'd stripped to his boxers, Sand flopped on the king-sized bed and awaited his turn to become human again.

He almost fell asleep. The curtains were closed, so no Vegas nighttime skyline was there to distract him, and only the space-age gold-and-glass lamp was on, glowing a muted yellow. The hotel's fixtures leaned toward the modern, a six-drawer cherry wood dresser opposite the bed atop which a Philco Townhouse television perched. Johnny Carson would be on soon but the remote control gizmo on the nightstand didn't even tempt him.

He was just starting to drift away when his wife called from the bathroom: "Do you think Double M will be annoyed with us?"

His mouth had acquired as thick and bad a taste as if he'd been sleeping for hours. He sighed a yawn, or perhaps yawned a sigh, slid off the bed and padded in. She was nude as a grape but with considerably more curves as she leaned in, testing the water. A pin-up artist would have paid her handsomely for that pose.

Vargas or Petty, however, might well have omitted her shoulder holster on the counter next to the sink, or the muddy, bloody clothes in a pile on the floor. Still, she was breathtaking, her skin perfectly tanned except for the alabaster her bikini left behind, as if to emphasize those areas of her slender form that needed no emphasizing at all.

"'Annoyed' is his perpetual state," Sand said, then brushed his teeth, saying through some foaming Crest, "but why should he be any more so than usual?"

"We attracted attention." She seemed to be satisfied with the temperature of the shower spray. "Of course, it wasn't our fault. We just attended the party. We didn't throw it."

She stepped into the shower, closed the door. He looked at her through the translucent glass and then thought, *What the hell? I'm dirty too.*

He joined her and began soaping her back, no washcloth, just his hand and a complimentary Camay bar, which he reluctantly passed to her. Over the drilling water, he said, "We're already set to meet with him."

"It's gotten so late! He's not postponing?"

"No. I called. He'll want to explore just who those people were and who sent them."

She looked back at him, making a face.

He clarified: "The people with guns?"

"Yes, I was following. Just had soap in my eyes." She stopped soaping herself for a second, thinking about it. "Could have been any one of a number of folks who want you dead."

"It is a rather long list," he admitted.

Passing him back the soap, turning to him, she said, "Even so, I would put Milan Meier at the top of that list."

Meier was the Dutch energy industrialist who last year had befriended the Sands on the island of Curaçao only to turn out to be a uranium smuggler. Additionally there was the small matter of Meier luring the couple into the hands of a mortal enemy with the idea that they would be killed, leaving the industrialist with credible deniability. They had upended Meier's plans, however, and their mortal enemy's, by surviving.

"Meier's at the top of the list," he agreed, over the drumming water, "with a star next to his name. You'll recall our brief ride from your training ground to the diner."

He soaped her breasts, just trying to be helpful.

"Vividly," she said. "You almost blew my scarf off."

"We weren't followed?"

"We were not followed."

They did not make love in the shower. He thought about it, and he sensed her thinking about it, too. But they had done that from time to time, and it always sounded better as a concept than an experience. So they toweled off and, wordlessly, walked naked into the bedroom and made very traditional, married-person, Missionary-position love, although with a frantic intensity born of nearly being assassinated not long before.

A while later, in Destiny Hotel robes, they were on the bed again, on their backs, side by side, and Sand was successfully resisting lighting up a *Gauloises*, out of respect to his bride of almost two years.

She asked, "How did they know where we were? How could they have been so well-prepared? Even the cook, the waitress..."

"I shared our plans with no one." Just a hint of accusation was in that.

She smirked at him. "Well, we've neither of us made any secret of it...your 'Friday special' at Moapa Diner."

"That's true. Still..."

The color drained from her face. "Ronald Kisor."

"Your firearms instructor. The Hogan's Alley adjudicator. The one who failed you?"

Her frown seemed mostly thoughtful. "He didn't fail

me—*I* failed me. But...we *did* talk about where you and I planned to dine. In fact, he appeared to know about that already. He even seemed familiar with the diner."

Sand smiled. "And that's how we make Double M annoyed with someone else, himself perhaps. We give him the mole who grassed."

"Who what?"

"Grassed—what's the American term? Ratted us out." He checked his Cortébert watch, which he'd collected from the wrist of a dead adversary. "We'd best get dressed and get upstairs."

Fifteen minutes later, Sand—in a navy-blue suit, white shirt, and crisply knotted blue-striped tie—and Stacey—in a peach-colored skirt-suit with a pale yellow silk blouse—made their elegant way to the elevators. A single elevator door, off to one side, lacked even an UP or DOWN button. Sand inserted a stubby key into a camlock, turned it slightly and the door whispered open. He extracted the key and they entered the car, where Sand pushed the second blue button in a vertical row of an unmarked three. The door slid shut, and they rose quickly to the nineteenth floor.

The floor below housed laboratories, computers and an arsenal, among much else, while this floor was given over to conference rooms and a warren of offices and workspace for agents, along with a decent-sized reference library. Both floors had a gray institutional blandness that could have served a school or an insurance firm, although those at least would have had something on the walls besides doorways. If anywhere in Las Vegas looked less like Las Vegas, Sand had not encountered it.

When the elevator doors whisked open, they stepped out into a bulletproof-glassed-in enclosure with a door on the facing glass wall, beyond which two agents book-ended the door through which the Sands would need to go. These watchdogs, one brown-haired, one blond, wore black suits, which went well with the lightweight Heckler & Koch MP5 submachine guns they cradled. Sand nodded to them and received nods back but no help with entry. At their door, he pressed his thumb to a scanner and a light turned green, though the door did not open. Stacey followed suit, and again the light turned green. Beyond the glass, the blond agent pressed a button and the door buzzed open. The couple stepped through and the door closed immediately, having the courtesy of not slamming itself.

Sand said, "Evening, Hans. Jake." As always, he couldn't help but think of Jake as "Fritz."

Jake Bowman, the brunette, considered smiling and didn't. "Mr. Sand."

The blond one, Hans Mueller, did smile, if almost imperceptibly, acknowledging Stacey. *"Guten abend, Frau Sand."*

She bequeathed him a much more generous smile. "Good evening, Hans."

Bowman said, "You're expected, John."

"Thanks."

Ahead of them was another door, this one unmarked. A dozen or so more were down the corridor to their left, but this was the one they needed. Sand opened it, held it for Stacey and they entered a small outer office. As anonymously gray as the rest of GUILE HQ, it at least bore sleek blond furniture and no sign of Double M's MI6 majordomo, the severe Mrs. Kitty Cash. This female guard at the gate was perhaps a hundred years younger than Sand's former nemesis, and a thousand times more cheerful.

An agent from Winnipeg, Maggie Bishop had been

assigned to GUILE as part of the Canadian contingent, even though the wounds she received on a UN mission had left her with a permanent limp and no chance of returning to the field. The pretty, red-headed widow had been part of the team investigating the plane crash in Northern Rhodesia in 1961 that killed sixteen including Secretary-General of the United Nations Dag Hammarskjöld. Now she enjoyed a position as Double M's personal assistant, if working with that brilliant but terminally grumpy boss could be deemed in any way enjoyable.

Maggie smiled sympathetically at the couple. "If you've never dealt with him this late in the day, you are in for a treat."

Sand said, "I hope we're not responsible for you having to stay after school."

She chuckled. "Littering a diner with eleven dead? You're barely in today's top five. Go right in."

They passed through the outer office and into the kingdom of Lord Malcolm Marbury, Double M, head of GUILE and former chief of MI6. This office was an exception to the gray hallways of the Global Unit headquarters, specifically designed to be a near match to their superior's former digs in London. Bookshelves lined oak-paneled walls, a huge global map all but engulfed the wall to the left as you came in, with only the bullet-proof picture window onto the neon garden of the Las Vegas strip to tell you this wasn't London.

Had Marbury's desk been any larger, Sand thought, it might require one of those new Zip Codes the American postal service threatened to implement. In a leather chair, essentially a throne that rocked and swiveled, sat Double M, his eyes cast down onto a report illuminated by a green-shaded banker's lamp, a big telephone/intercom system nearby representing modernity encroaching upon this Churchillian domain. Two straight-back dark-wooden chairs awaited them in front of the desk, looking as comfortable as Calvinist church pews. The couple did not sit down, instead standing behind the chairs.

Though his former MI6 chief had always reminded Sand of a slightly fleshier Noel Coward, from a receding hairline to an upper-crust demeanor, Sand had never shared this observation with the man himself—never having had a desire to be posted in Antarctica.

Tonight, the Director of the Global Unit wore an impeccably gray Savile Row suit with a gold watch chain draping the matching vest, school cufflinks in place on a starched white shirt, and silk light-blue-stripe-on-a-black-background Eton tie, perfectly knotted. Without looking up, he said, "How did you allow this to happen, Triple Seven?"

Marbury insisted on continuing to use Sand's old MI6 numerical designation.

But before the agent could reply, Stacey said, "*I* may have allowed it to happen. Frankly, sir, I was indiscreet."

Double M's ocean-blue eyes took on an icy cast rising slowly from the report to Stacey, then to Sand, and back again. "Elaborate, if you would."

"I mentioned our dining plans to my firearms instructor—Ronald Kisor. That's less than an accusation, understand, but it's a leak I can trace."

Turning his attention to Sand, Double M said, "The two of you killed eleven people. You do realize your liquidate-without-prejudice classification does not transfer from MI6 to our new multi-national organization, hmmm?"

"I do, sir. But circumstances rated a response. If you like, I can report in detail, sir."

"Later. For now, I've gotten the gist from speaking with the local officials who were less than chuffed to be sidelined by a call from a certain high-ranking member of the Justice Department."

Attorney General was as high-ranking as it got.

"Here are the issues facing me," Marbury said wearily. "You two continue to behave in a manner demonstrating bravery and resourcefulness, but also a recklessness that can't be countenanced. Additionally, you're well-known, even famous, in these united states at least. And celebrity is not helpful in an endeavor as circumspect as our own."

"You left out 'effective,'" Sand said, "in delineating our behavior."

Double M rolled his head slightly, which generally indicated an effort to control his words. "Which is why I'm not sacking the both of you right now."

Stacey said, "It was a well-organized attack, sir. An elaborate, carefully planned and staged assassination attempt."

The GUILE director nodded slowly. "Planned and staged by whom, would you say?"

Sand said, "We believe the likeliest candidate to be Milan Meier."

"I don't disagree. If so, by now Meier has found out that his assassins have failed. Which leaves him where?"

With a shrug Sand said, "To come at us again."

"Undoubtedly. But we'll get to that. First, I need to address Mrs. Sand...Sit down, both of you. I prefer eyes at a level."

They did, Sand struck by that old called-to-the-school-master's-office feeling.

"Mrs. Sand...I am frankly not convinced you are ready for a field assignment—at least, not a dangerous and/or sensitive one."

"Call me 'Stacey,' please. After all, I *did* save your life last year. In the field?"

Sand repressed a smile; he loved her for the understated cheekiness of that. And a thousand other things.

Even Double M couldn't hold back a smile. "That little favor you did me," he said, "is a good part of why I am *not* sacking you. However, Mrs. Sand, *Stacey,* I understand that you did not achieve the necessarily perfect score on the so-called 'Hogan's Alley' gauntlet."

Her chin came up slightly. "I did not," she confirmed. "But aside from that one misstep, my scores are higher than any other candidate in my group."

"That one misstep—failing to recognize and terminate an enemy agent—could have cost you your life, and that of anyone working with you. Then you compounded that failure by demonstrating a lack of discretion with Kisor."

Sand sat forward. "You spoke with him? He told you personally that my wife failed that test?"

Double M raised a hand. "Sending over that score appears to be the last thing Agent Kisor did prior to...well, going AWOL, one might say. He was not at his apartment, leaving indications of a hurried departure. We are...looking into it further. It may be innocent enough. He may have made plans for the weekend."

"He's in the wind," Sand said. "GUILE allowed a mole in among us. You're lucky we didn't have another disastrous raid right here. How many lives were lost in that last debacle...sir?"

Marbury bristled, but said nothing.

Sand went on: "My wife has demonstrated her skills under fire...last year in Curaçao, and today in that diner... showing she has what it takes to make it in your precious 'field.' Overlooking one dummy in that gauntlet of yours is a misdemeanor. GUILE allowing that traitor in the house is a felony."

Sand got to his feet and held his hand out to his wife.

"We're done here," he said.

Stacey rose, but—almost shockingly—so did Double M.

"Sit down, please," he said. His voice was soft, damn near gentle. His hands patted the air.

Sand glanced at Stacey and she glanced back. Then she sat and so did he.

"As I said," the Director continued, "I don't doubt your bravery or your resourcefulness." He was speaking to both of them. "And you have demonstrated considerable skills, Mrs. Sand...Stacey...particularly for a candidate with no background in law enforcement or tradecraft. On the other hand, your position as a CEO of a major company...and yours, John, as that woman's husband, and the man who unfortunately is the most famous spy in the world right now...limits your usefulness. But not necessarily your effectiveness."

Sand said, "Explain."

"As oil company executives, you provide each other with a perfect cover, and an entrée into circles few can manage. So we must be selective, and careful, in how we utilize you and your positions...your celebrity...your access to the highest ranks of power, of government, of commerce."

"Am I," Stacey said quietly, "or am I not an agent? Or simply a 'candidate'...or perhaps, what is the word? An 'asset?'"

"You're an agent, Stacey. Like John, you'll be offered a dollar a year for the honor."

That got smiles out of them.

"You will both be, shall we say, working parttime.

When needed. When your talents and positions are called for. After all, you two can't be gallivanting around the globe when you have an oil company to run."

"Energy company," she corrected.

But Double M was right, Sand knew. His wife had a board of directors, and a cadre of trusted executives; but Boldt Energy was her baby, and even her executive vice president—her husband—didn't make a move without consulting her.

"And as it happens," Double M said, "your talents and connections *are* called for...and right now."

They exchanged glances as the Director flipped open a file folder.

"When we returned from Curaçao, Triple Seven," Double M said, "your report mentioned an acquaintance of Meier's—a certain 'Petrus.'"

"Yes, sir. That's his last name, apparently. Didn't catch a given one. Older gent, business partner or employee of Meier's, perhaps. As you know, I helped with an artist's rendering, which I think was spot on."

"I hope so. Because based upon that, there have been possible sightings in Brazil."

Sand flashed a grin at Stacey. "Brazil should make a nice getaway for a wealthy young couple." To Marbury he said, "When do we leave?"

"John, you're flying to São Paulo tomorrow to see if you can find this Petrus. Support is waiting. Some actual spying might be possible, as you're not as well-known there as you are here."

"*I'm* known to Meier."

Double M nodded. "And if he's in São Paulo or else-where in Brazil, your presence may well draw him out."

Stacey said, "Why not send me along, then? I can recognize Meier, too, and we could be a vacationing couple...."

Double M stopped her with a raised palm. "I have something else for you, Stacey. You wanted a field assignment? Well, I have one for which you are uniquely qualified—there's a United Nations energy conference coming up..."

"Geneva," she cut in with a nod. "I'm already scheduled to attend, as a representative of Boldt Energy, of course."

"And now you'll also be attending as an agent of GUILE. You just won't be advertising it."

Marbury withdrew a photo from his folder and pushed it across the desk between the Sands—a surveillance shot of two men engaged in conversation at an outdoor café.

Double M asked, "Either of these a familiar face?"

The forty-something man on the right, who Sand recognized at once, was bald, looked fit, and wore a dark well-tailored suit. The other gentleman looked younger, paunchier, his dark hair swept back, his suit expensive, too; he wore sunglasses—Persol 714s. In the black-and-white print only their pale skin was apparent, no discerning eye color or even exact hair color.

Stacey tapped the bald man's picture. "Florin Covaci, Romanian Minister of Energy. I don't know his friend. John?"

Sand said, "I recognize Covaci, too, but not the other."

"You've encountered Covaci?" Double M asked her.

Stacey shook her head. "I know who he is. I make it a point with potential Boldt Energy buyers."

"The man neither of you recognize has been identified as Michel Hearn. New on the scene, an Argentine of German heritage. We know little about him but, like Meier, he's been sniffing around for uranium."

Stacey frowned in thought. "A surrogate for Meier,

perhaps?"

Both men looked at her.

She explained: "Covaci is energy minister of Romania, a country with a border on the Black Sea. If Covaci is selling uranium, instead of buying, and doing so behind the government's back? Getting it out of the country wouldn't be that difficult."

Double M said, "*That* is why you're going to Geneva, Stacey. Hearn will be there—you're to determine what it is he's up to."

Sand said, "Wouldn't it be better if Stacey's first field assignment was at my side?"

"I'm not sending her alone." Touching a button on the intercom. "Miss Bishop, has the agent arrived?"

"Yes, sir."

"Send her in, please," Double M said, then clicked off.

Charlotte DuBois, an agent Sand knew well—including in the Biblical sense—entered with fluid grace, as lovely as ever. In a cream-colored suit, her long-legged Bardot body seemed apparently none the worse for wear after the wounds she'd suffered in the raid on the former GUILE HQ, when Sand had seen her last. She crossed the room to him, dark hair flouncing.

He got to his feet and she gave him a comradely hug as he kissed her on both cheeks. "You look well!" Sand said. "Lord Marbury told me you'd fully recovered, but I didn't know you were back on the job."

"You got me to the hospital just in time, *mon ami*, the doctors say."

He was relieved she did not say "*mon amour*" as she had so often before.

Stacey was standing, too, smiling, though there was some strain in it. He had told her about Charlotte. Some of it, anyway. He introduced them.

Stacey passed on kissing the woman's cheeks and they shook hands in an overtly masculine manner.

"Charlotte, I've heard so much about you," Stacey said. "But John didn't tell me you were this beautiful."

"Ah, but he told me how *magnifique* you are," the brunette said, "and he did not exaggerate."

Sand gave Double M a dirty look. Double M wore a smugly satisfied smile. Did the Director of GUILE realize that these were the only two women in the world who John Sand had ever asked to marry him?

CHAPTER THREE
CONVENTIONAL BEHAVIOR

———

The Beau-Rivage Genève, one of Switzerland's oldest hotels, had been founded by the Mayer family in 1865, with the wealthy in mind. Now, nearly a hundred years later, the five-star luxury destination in Geneva continued to seek just such a clientele, among whom oil heiress Stacey Sand certainly qualified.

Yet rich kid Stacey had rarely traveled outside the confines of the continental United States, and these swank surroundings—she and Charlotte DuBois occupied two of the hotel's ninety rooms, with adjoining doors—fairly overwhelmed the Texas girl.

Stacey's room was wider than it was long, with two lavender-draped picture windows separated by a working marble fireplace providing a picture postcard view of the Rhône emptying out of Lake Geneva. The walls were pale green linen wallpaper within white molding, with occasional framed black-and-white photographs of the hotel's storied history; a double bed, over whose foot hung a crystal chandelier, included pale green scalloped frame and a padded headboard encased in lavender silk.

Elegant furnishings lurked in every corner, reading tables with mounted lamps, an ebony desk, even the bathroom door offering a stained-glass geometric design. The Hilton hotels she and John frequented back in the states could hardly hope to compete.

As for her almost roommate next door, Stacey didn't feel she needed a babysitter, or more accurately a body-guard—particularly when that guard's body belonged to a beautiful woman who had a history with John Sand.

Stacey's husband had been frank if vague about that ("Charlotte and I worked together in dangerous circum-stances, and grew close for a time"). Not that Marbury had given Mrs. Sand any choice in the matter, and then there was the concern in her husband's eyes, which convinced Stacey any further objection would be fruitless.

John's worry for her summoned a contradictory re-sponse—Stacey felt at once closer to him, and yet further apart. This man had married into her family's business and swiftly learned how to make himself an asset in her world. But she had married into *his* business too, entering *his* world, and however quick a learner she might be, the young woman lacked his lifetime of experience as a pro-fessional in espionage.

In her trade, a mistake meant a monetary loss that might impact not only her life but that of thousands of share-holders. In his, losses were numbered in lives, not dollars, and not just those of agents—one mistake could mean the deaths of hundreds, thousands, even millions... That ex-plained the loving yet haunted look in her husband's dark blue eyes, which had muted her objections to Charlotte DuBois accompanying her to the Geneva gathering.

Now, a mere two days after that meeting with Marbury (and Charlotte DuBois), Stacey took one last appraising look at herself in the elaborately framed fireplace mirror. Her hair and makeup were properly understated—the hotel beauty shop had done well by her—her navy-blue Givenchy suit suitably business-like smart. Her only concession had been to comfort—Bass Weejun spectator pumps with low chunky heels, reflecting the number of steps she anticipated walking today. She smiled and the magnate in the mirror smiled back.

A knock came at the adjoining door; she went over and admitted Charlotte. Wearing a gray suit (Chanel) and carrying a gray leather purse over a shoulder (Gucci?) and a binder under an arm, Charlotte looked perfectly appropriate for her role as Stacey's personal assistant. With Boldt Energy growing as a global energy provider, its CEO having an assistant who spoke French only made sense, especially here in Geneva where over a fifth of the population spoke the language.

"Good morning, Mrs. Sand," Charlotte said, although the women addressed each other by their first names after business hours. "Our car is waiting downstairs."

"Thank you, Miss DuBois," Stacey said. "I'll just grab my purse." Which she did—like Charlotte, Stacey utilized a shoulder bag to leave her hands free (both women had pistols in their purses). She also picked up a zippered portfolio with a blank tablet and a Mont Blanc pen.

Within minutes they were exiting the ornate lobby into the bright sun of a June Geneva morning. A gray Mercedes sedan drew up, the uniformed doorman ushering them into the commodious back seat and closing them in with a smile and no expectation of a tip till the end of their stay.

The driver, whose gray suit matched his vehicle as opposed to the usual chauffeur's livery, was in his late twenties, his hair a light brown, his dark brown eyes meeting Stacey's warmly in the rearview mirror.

"Good morning, Mrs. Sand," he said, his accent a lightly accented British. "I'm Joseph."

"Good morning, Joseph."

Then, with a smile and nod into the rearview, he added, "I have ordered up a nice morning for you, Charlotte."

Charlotte, with perhaps a hint of flirtation (although with the French woman that was hard to tell), said, "Very thoughtful of you, Joseph."

Stacey asked softly, "One of yours?"

"One of *ours, mon chéri.* Joseph is a GUILE agent stationed in Geneva."

As the car rolled away from the hotel, Stacey asked, "With at least one of 'ours' already posted here, why were you sent along?"

"Because I have a certain familiarity with you and your habits."

Taken aback but not showing it, Stacey said, "Why would that be?"

Charlotte was regarding the passing cityscape out the window. "Last year, when you were in Brownsville, Texas, and decided to run off in pursuit of your father's betrayer, I was the one who lost you when you crossed over into Mexico. I vowed I would never fail to protect you again."

Stacey paused to blink, then asked, "Vowed to John or to Lord Marbury?"

"*Oui,*" Charlotte said simply.

Stacey studied the French woman for a long moment, then said, with the smallest touch of sarcasm, "*Merci.*"

Joseph drove the three kilometers to Ariana Park and *Palais des Nations.* Built between 1929 and 1938 as a monument to peace, the massive whitestone Art Deco complex, originally housing the League of Nations, was now

European headquarters of the United Nations. Naturally, the UN Energy Conference was being held within several of its many conference rooms, where panels of experts, industrialists and political leaders would discuss oil, coal, natural gas, and nuclear energy, the latter being the reason Stacey and her assistant were in attendance.

With such a long line of cars pulling in, it took a while for their driver to deposit them at the main entrance, assuring his passengers he would be nearby at all times.

Stacey and Charlotte stepped into the bright sun and made the short walk to the row of glass doors. While security would surely be high, no armed guards were in sight. Behind her, a smoothly Slavic voice, a bit reminiscent of Bela Lugosi, said, "Allow me, please."

A bald man wearing a well-cut navy-blue suit and a distinguished air, but no overcoat, materialized, extending his arm toward the door the two women approached. His aide was trotting to catch up.

"Thank you, Minister Covaci," Stacey said, with a generous smile and modest nod.

His nod, as he pushed open the door, was similarly modest but his smile was even more generous. "The lovely Mrs. Sand honors me with her recognition. But I would surely recall if we had ever met."

"This is our first meeting," Stacey said, another nod, another smile, then she was through the door with Charlotte trailing respectfully after.

As Covaci's young, nondescript male aide took over doorman duties, his boss fell in beside Charlotte and followed Stacey into a spacious lobby abuzz with attendee conversations.

Covaci moved up alongside Stacey. "Would it be rude of me to inquire how it is you might recognize a minor

Romanian official?"

On Stacey's other side now, Charlotte said, "I will take care of registration, Mrs. Sand."

"Thank you, Miss DuBois," Stacey said, as the French agent peeled off toward a row of tables with attendees checking in—mostly men. The occasional assistant like Charlotte aside, Stacey would appear to be one of perhaps half a dozen females here.

To Covaci, she said, "You are too modest, Minister. You procure energy for your country, after all—and I *sell* energy."

Covaci chuckled. "They say the women of Texas are, like the men, straight shooters. I can see I have not been misinformed."

"I prefer doing business with well-informed, uh... individuals." Her half smile elicited a big smile from the minister, who obviously understood she had purposefully said "individuals" not "men."

And of course she didn't lower herself to asking how Covaci recognized her. She and John had garnered enough publicity as a couple to make her quite accustomed to strangers knowing who she was—the youngest female CEO in the States, and married to the spy whose author friend had made a fortune out of exaggerating his former colleague's exploits.

As Charlotte returned with her arms full of folders and handouts, an almost leering Covaci said, "And I, for a change, look forward to entering negotiations with an 'individual' graced with such feminine charms."

Apparently proud of himself, he moved quickly away, his assistant rushing to keep up.

Stacey found this kind of knee-jerk flirtation typical of the powerful men she'd met since assuming control of

Boldt Oil. They always seemed to have to take their shot, assuming that because she had the temerity to enter their realm, sexual one-upmanship would affirm their rightful position—on top, of course. At least *her* man enjoyed being on the bottom when the mood struck.

"Interesting accent," Charlotte said, an eyebrow raised.

"*Transylvanian*, from the sound of it," Stacey said.

Going through the registration materials, Charlotte said, "You would think the United Nations might do better than stick-on name tags."

"Men have limited imaginations," Stacey said.

Her assistant shrugged. "*Some* men." She applied her name tag and Stacey's, defiling their fashionable attire. Stacey's eyes were following Covaci's retreat, in case possible black market uranium buyer Michel Hearn came along to join his friend. Who knew? She might get lucky and trip over her prey while still in the lobby.

But no sign availed itself of the German-pedigree Argentinian, not in Covaci's company or anywhere else she could see. Charlotte was distributing handout materials between them—timetables, panel information, room numbers—saying, "We're in the Council Chamber." She indicated a massive triptych over double glass doors.

The marble bas-relief—*The Creation of Man*—featured a reclining figure in its sweeping center panel, inspired by Michelangelo's Sistine Chapel fresco. On either side smaller panels illustrated *Man's Gifts to God* and *God's Gifts to Man*. Stacey, who'd only ever experienced sculptor Eric Gill's artwork in books, was deeply moved by the sculpture, a gift from the United Kingdom to the League of Nations in 1938.

Somehow it spoke to the larger mission of the work she was taking on with John—adventure, excitement, adrenalin rush, all were empty things without some sense of accomplishment for a greater good.

But a few moments of admiring the sculpture, and reflecting upon it, were quickly over as she continued to discreetly stay on the watch for Michel Hearn. Ever more attendees—again, men mostly—were streaming in, and those already registered were moving toward their particular panel or meeting now. Important people, famous people, were caught up in the anonymous indignity of a crowd. Spotting one man she had never met among this horde was perhaps a task whose hope of success was improbable if not impossible. The volume of ambient conversations rose with the number of new conferees in the lobby until the whole place was a buzzing, busy hive.

Not losing Charlotte in the madness was difficult enough without searching as many faces as possible see if Hearn's was one of them. That these were chiefly corporate gray-flannel drones didn't help, hair varying little in cut and only in color and thinness or absence. Though she and Charlotte were lonely flowers in this desert, most of these bees were concentrating on whatever their purpose was for being here, attractive honey drawing only a few appreciate smiles before being swept back up in the swarm.

None of them Michel Hearn.

The two women finally made their way into the Council Chamber and selected aisle seats toward the back, where Stacey would be better able to survey the crowd. Though lacking an angle on the balcony, Stacey figured if Hearn wasn't on the main floor, she and Charlotte would simply slip out early and watch attendees exiting down the balcony stairs.

In tiered theater-style seating, the two hundred attendees faced a C-shaped table large enough to accommodate two dozen people. She slowly scanned the room, which was already filling up. No sign of her man among the many.

Then, emerging from a side door, came an individual whose slight heaviness was mitigated by a navy-blue suit noticeably well-tailored even in this company; his white shirt stiffly starched, silk ascot tied at the open throat, he wore glasses tinted almost to the degree of her husband's Ray-Bans. Moving gracefully for a paunchy man, he assumed the big table's central seat, where he sat and leaned into his microphone.

"Good morning. My name, as a few of you already know, is Michel Hearn. I am a native of Argentina...and I am here to talk to you about freedom."

He had the crowd's attention now, Stacey included. Some even were sitting forward, and more than a few looked ready to clap, though applause did not quite happen.

"The freedom that comes with mastering the power of the atom," he said in a smooth baritone with a lightly Latin accent. "I am speaking, of course, of nuclear energy."

He withdrew the microphone from its holder, got to his feet, stepped away from the table just enough to pace as he spoke. "The power of the atom is clearly the future. It will liberate the citizens of the world, enabling them to taste the freedoms that most of us in this room already enjoy. The harnessed atom will lift humanity to the next level of existence. And for the next thousand years, with war robbed of its reason for existence, peace will reign."

This man's voice was deeper, his accent leaning toward Spanish not Dutch of course, but Stacey made the connection, all right. Hearn was about the correct height. His hair was brown and parted on the side where Meier's had been prematurely white and combed straight back. Meier had been fit and this man was generally heavier, and was Dutch, this Argentinian's skin tone darker than the Dutchman's, the features subtly different...

...but the words, the concepts expressed, were almost identical to what Stacey had heard in Curaçao.

She was right. She knew it. Lacking proof, operating primarily from her gut, she nonetheless had no doubt.

Stacey Sand, Charlotte DuBois, and everyone in this room—many of them powerful, all of them in some manner or form influential—was listening to Milan Meier.

* * * * * *

Flying to Sâo Paulo, Brazil, to pick up the trail of Petrus, an apparent significant business associate of Milan Meier, might have seemed a routine enough job for the experienced likes of John Sand. But that single name was about all Sand had to go on in a city with a population of nearly five million people, including large numbers of Portuguese, Spanish, Italian, and Greek immigrants who'd come to work in Brazil's factories.

He'd looked for needles in well-populated haystacks before, and with a search that had begun worldwide, GUILE had at least narrowed the global haystack to Sâo Paulo.

Upon landing at Congonhas Airport, Sand was not unpleasantly surprised to find Phillip Lyman waiting for him in the terminal. The blond, tan, blue-eyed Lyman might have been a mildly ageing surfer who'd lost his way from some California beach; his white suit with a white shirt and a baby-blue tie could have belonged to a tourist or a businessman. Instead, he was Sand's longtime and highly valued CIA contact, and that big, white, familiar smile as Sand approached spoke of their long friendship.

Sand unleashed a grin of his own as he extended

his hand. "Phillip, you've come a long way to work on your tan."

For the benefit of anyone pretending not to be interested, Lyman said, "Always ready to go out of the way for an old pal." Then, as the pair shook hands and moved closer, he added, sotto voce, "And anyway, I've been ordered by the powers-that-be to cooperate with GUILE."

"You always operated with guile," Sand said, softly. "It just wasn't an organization yet. Would you be who spotted the, uh, friend of a friend?"

Lyman shook his head and the two men fell into silence as they walked through the crowded concourse. Outside, in a warm buttery sun, they bypassed a row of taxis and Sand tagged along with his friend to a nearby parking lot and a black Ford sedan.

With Lyman behind the wheel and Sand in the passenger seat, they both immediately rolled down their windows, and Sand got out of his light sports jacket, tailored to conceal his shoulder rig, and was down to a lime Ban-Lon and darker green slacks. As usual for São Paulo this time of year, the temperature was in the seventies, the sun wide and high in a cloudless sky, a whisper of breeze offering the only respite from the heat.

They were out of the lot before Lyman spoke again. "I'm not the one who spotted Petrus—one of our operatives did. He contacted me and I contacted the Director, who handed me off to your Double M. And here we are, in a sunny vacation clime."

"Looking for a potential uranium smuggler."

"It's a living."

"If you refer to the smuggler, it is until we catch up with him. If you're referring to those of us seeking such smugglers, we're fine as long as we don't glow in the dark when we switch off the light at bedtime."

They maneuvered into traffic and Sand paid scant attention to where they were going. São Paulo was massive, and growing at a frightening rate, having more than doubled in a decade or so. A month ago, the city had hosted the Pan American Games, the Olympics-style athletic event featuring teams from all the countries of the Americas, held every four years, a year before the Olympics. Sâo Paulo was truly a metropolis now, thanks in part to the international exposure the Pan Am Games had given it.

Sand said, "I'd like to talk to the agent who spotted Petrus, if that's permitted."

"That's who we're going to see now. He's a Brazilian who works for us here. By the way, John, Petrus isn't the friend-of-a-friend's real name."

"Do tell."

Lyman grinned over at him. "Once I saw the surveillance photo, bells began to ring in this crude but sometimes useful computer between my ears. 'Petrus,' it turns out, is really one Johan Nielsen. That ring any of your bells?"

Something indeed was chiming. "There was a Johan Nielsen who was an SS officer—worked under Heinrich Himmler himself. One of his aides, I believe."

"An interest in Nazi history," Lyman said with a wry chuckle, "does come in handy now and then, in our line of work."

With a thoughtful frown, Sand said, "Meier strikes me as an idealist gotten out of hand, an ends-justifies-the-means character if the means seem to him to lead to the greater good. In which case one must wonder—what the hell was he doing meeting with an ex-Nazi?"

Lyman, steering with his left hand, shrugged with his right shoulder. "Maybe he didn't realize that was what he was doing. Or, looking to buy black market uranium, maybe Meier didn't care who was peddling it. Ends justifies the means, remember?"

"He'd know who he was dealing with, of that I'm convinced. This geezer knew we were changing our name to Boldt Energy before we went public with it. He practically bragged about knowing everything about everyone in his circle...or who might be asked to enter it. How did you confirm Nielsen's identity?"

Another one-shoulder shrug. "Once we realized this was the guy you were looking for, we followed him, got a drinking glass with a fingerprint, and—what is it you Brits say? 'Bob's your uncle.'"

"And what is it you Yanks say—it's a 'lead-pipe cinch' Meier knew about Nielsen's past. Question is, was Meier in bed with Nielsen *in spite* of his Nazi past... or because of it?"

Traffic was moving slowly now, as Lyman edged them toward the outer districts. He said, "You saw them together on Curaçao—Meier and Nielsen?"

"I did."

Casually, Lyman observed, "Curaçao is less than five hundred miles from Venezuela, you know."

"Always grateful for a geography refresher, Phillip. It's been ages since Cambridge. What are you getting at?"

"Just one further geographic note—Venezuela is in South America."

"The rest of this lesson," Sand said, "you can skip."

Both agents knew all too well that South America was home to a seemingly endless array of escaped Nazis.

"You're the one who spent time with Meier," Lyman said. "Is it credible he'd become involved in a scheme involving former Nazis? If there's even any 'former' about it."

"Nazis are the opposite of what he waxed eloquent about to Stacey and myself. He spoke of freedom for all men. But such an alliance brings us back to my initial point."

"The end," Lyman said, "justifying the means."

The CIA agent wheeled the Ford onto a narrow side street and parked. Sand slipped the sports jacket back on—wouldn't do to have the Walther sticking its butt into things. When they emerged from the vehicle, he smiled, his senses pleasantly assaulted by the aroma of spicy cooking from an open second-floor window of the stone building next to him. The best thing about international travel, Sand knew, was the food. He followed Lyman back to Rua Augusta, the wider, busier street from which they'd turned off. Traffic was still heavy, and little better on the sidewalk.

Lyman said, "So Meier is all in favor of peace on earth and good will for men. Christmas every day, hallelujah, Amen. And no one up to no good ever lied about their intentions, right?"

Sand, considering that a rhetorical question, said, "Meier seemed sincere enough, right up to when he sent Stacey and me into a murder trap. My question is, are his intentions—whatever they might be—merely acquiring uranium from any old source, or does he have any other link to Nielsen and assorted surviving Nazis?"

"Such as a shared goal?"

"Such as a shared goal. And I don't believe the Nazis are interested in Christmas coming on a daily basis... Where are we walking to, incidentally? Or do you simply like spending time with me?"

"Over there," Lyman said, pointing across the busy street to an outdoor café on the next corner. A dozen or so small round tables, surrounded by rattan chairs, were taken by men in white or beige suits, drinking coffee, many smoking cigars. A very few women were scattered around as attractive window dressing. And, at one of these tables, Sand spotted his quarry—Petrus aka Johan Nielsen, who had changed little if at all since their brief encounter at Milan Meier's mansion, *Landhuis Paradijs,* on Curaçao.

As before, Johan Nielsen seemed in fine shape for a man in his sixties, though his hair, graying at the temples, was skimpy up top, which clipped-close barbering did not disguise; his eyebrows threatened to overwhelm eyes slitted against the sun. Like Lyman, Nielsen wore a white suit and shirt, though his tie was a muted red. A Panama hat rested on the table near his left hand, his right bearing a cigarette in a holder.

Nielsen shared the table with two others, a broad-shouldered man with the look of a military man gone somewhat to seed—a bodyguard? A gun for hire? The woman, from this distance anyway, bore a resemblance to Kyla Fluss, Milan Meier's seductive hired hand, who Agent Triple Seven had first met in 1959 while he was still on her Majesty's payroll and the German agent on the highest bidder's.

Of course, this woman had brown hair while Kyla was a blonde, naturally so, as Sand determined when they'd first rubbed shoulders, among other things. From here, anyway, the woman appeared somewhat younger than Kyla, if every bit as bosomy. If she was Fluss, what a bonus that would be to finding "Petrus," further connecting him to Meier.

"Make him?" Lyman asked.

"Oh yes."

"Two tables further right? That's our man Cristiano."

Sand nodded.

The three at Nielsen's table appeared to be in deep conversation, the possible Kyla Fluss included. This would take finesse. Sand wanted to get close enough to eavesdrop without being made.

"Phillip, can you catch a ride with Cristiano?"

"Probably—why?"

"I'm moving closer, and if Nielsen leaves, I may need a car."

"My car, of course," Lyman said, as if surprised it had taken this long for Sand to impose in some manner. "And you'd like me to move it closer, too, I suppose?"

"With that psychic ability, Phillip, you should hold seances. The next side street over will do nicely."

"I'll do that," Lyman said. "And if things go poorly, John, be sure to send me a message from the next world.... The keys will be on the visor."

"I'm sure Double M will send along a nice thank you note."

"Something to look forward to." He put a hand on his friend's shoulder. "Good hunting."

Then the CIA agent turned and walked back in the direction they'd come, threading through heavy pedestrian traffic.

Across the way Nielsen and his guests were still in conversation. Sand started across, hoping to find a table well-positioned for him to learn what a high-ranking former Nazi might be up to these days.

CHAPTER FOUR
DOCTOR, DOCTOR

Sand crossed through considerable traffic onto a similarly clogged sidewalk just as the Johan Nielsen party began getting to their feet and making their goodbyes. Nielsen was headed away from him, and Sand tagged after, but suddenly the attractive brunette and the wide load accompanying her were coming right toward him, swimming against the pedestrian tide.

The bulky, burly character wore a dark off-the-rack suit, heat be damned, and a gray porkpie hat at least one size too small for that boulder of a skull sitting atop shoulders that neglected to provide him with a neck. The woman, near her escort's right, fractionally behind him, as he carved a path like a lineman in American football, wore a yellow curve-hugging sheath dress, not quite as bright as the sun.

Sand looked past the unlikely couple and Nielsen was still in sight, moving with the crowd, but just then the brunette bumped into him, all but walking into his arms.

"Pardon," Sand said automatically, the woman bracing herself on his biceps, as she stumbled.

Close-up, the resemblance to Kyla Fluss—unless

this *was* Kyla Fluss—seemed even more compelling, including similarly ample charms. But oversize sunglasses concealed eye color, and the tawny brown hair was a mane noticeably longer than Kyla ever wore, the nose and mouth different somehow. And this assaultively stunning creature seemed a bit younger than the German operative—mid-twenties, not thirties.

Still...could this be Kyla?

Then she spoke, working above the sidewalk murmur: "Oh darlin', I'm sorry, fault is mine, I'm such a clumsy child sometimes."

The Southern accent and the pitch of her voice were not at all Kyla. As the sidewalk crowd flowed around them like they were stones in a stream, she made no immediate move to extricate herself.

"Think I broke a heel," she said, off-balance, and he walked her to the edge of the café's outdoor seating, as passing pedestrians, chuckling, smiling, got a look at these two striking people. Her burly companion, who'd been a few steps ahead, wove his way back to them.

The tawny-haired beauty was adjusting her right shoe. "Oh, good. Just stepped out of it. I'm such a klutz, sometimes. Do you even understand a word I'm sayin', darlin'?"

"I speak American," he said and gave her a smile, but was looking past her, searching the crowd; Nielsen had disappeared.

The big guy was next to them now. "You all right, baby?"

"Fine," she assured him. "I'm Michelle Rivers and this is Rocky, my husband."

"Rocky Rivers?" Sand said, extending his hand. "Memorable."

The burly man shook the hand listlessly, tiny eyes

giving Sand a suspicious onceover.

"Rocky, this gentleman has been just that," the woman said. "A gentleman." To Sand she said, "You may *speak* American, honey, but that lovely accent says you're from somewhere else. British Isles, maybe?"

"London, mostly," Sand said. "Nice meeting you both, and I'm pleased your heel is fine." Whether he was referring to her shoe or her looming companion he left for Mrs. Rivers to navigate.

"Bumpin' into another nice out-of-towner like yourself is an unexpected pleasure, Mr., uh...sorry, what was your name again?"

No "again" about it, and that left him having to choose whether to offer an alias, or...and he heard himself saying, "Sand. John Sand."

She patted his cheek and said flirtatiously, "Well, a couple of rivers and one big handsome sandy shore. What fun."

And then the couple slipped back into the pedestrian stream, with a wink from her and a glare from him.

That *was* Kyla Fluss, damnit—wasn't it? The slight differences in age and facial features, the different hair color, the Southern accent, the husband, if that *was* a husband and not just a bodyguard... That *was* her!

Right?

And if so, should he follow her? With her connection to Meier, she'd make a worthwhile subject for surveillance, all right; and she had after all been talking to Nielsen, just a couple of Germanic peas in a pod.

Then a black Mercedes limousine rolled by.

At the wheel, a driver in cap and chauffeur's livery looked as blond and blandly handsome as if he dropped off a National Socialist Party recruiting poster. In the window behind the driver was the arrogant squashed oval of a face belonging to Johan Nielsen.

Dumb luck, but that was fine with Sand. The possible Kyla Fluss took an immediate figurative backseat to this man in a literal backseat.

That black Mercedes was heading back the way he and Lyman had originally come, which meant Sand might be able to retrieve his CIA friend's Ford before losing sight of Nielsen's limo. He slipped through the crowd to the side street where the unlocked black Ford awaited, its nose pointed toward busy Rua Augusta. As promised, the keys were on the visor. Soon he was pulling out into a cacophony of car horns and a dissonant chorus of obscenities in Portuguese and Spanish, with one English counterpoint suggesting Sand attempt something physically impossible if admirably ambitious.

The Ford had that crude muscularity of American cars, a horse constantly in danger of overrunning the fox. But the Mercedes was separated from it by a comfortable half dozen cars, so staying with the big sleek vehicle, unobtrusively, presented little problem. Sand was even able to keep up a concurrent search for the probable Kyla and her companion Rocky in the sidewalk crowd, though they seemed to have disappeared. Perhaps Lyman's man Cristano had displayed some initiative and followed them. Right now his only goal was not to lose sight of the big boxy black Mercedes with its distinctive chrome trim.

The limo kept heading north, the town's edge fast approaching, and Sand lost his cushion of cars as traffic thinned. Still, he was able to hang back at least two cars at all times, and did not appear to have been made, even after São Paulo was in the rearview mirrors.

He was relieved that Lyman's gas gauge indicated a

full tank, because as the city's buildings gave the way, the skyline became one of jungle-covered hills broken only by the occasional farm field. In these environs, the *agricultores* scraped out a living, claiming small patches of land from the surrounding jungle to grow coffee and a few vegetables.

Two hours passed before signs announced the close proximity of a bump in the road called Serra Negra. Shortly thereafter the Mercedes turned off the highway onto a dirt road leading up a hill to a weathered white-washed, tile-roofed brick farmhouse surrounded by jungle. Sand slowed slightly, just enough to clock the tail of the Mercedes, then kept going another kilometer till he could turn off onto a secondary road.

Unpaved, it was smooth enough to serve and no one else was around. Finding a clearing off to the left, he pulled in and parked as deep into the jungle shadows as he dared, then gathered some palm fronds and camouflaged the vehicle best as possible. Then, Walther P38 in hand, took off through the undergrowth back toward the farm; luck remained with him as the green of his jacket, shirt and slacks, even his sports sneakers, would help where he was heading.

So, possibly, would the Walther.

But that weapon wasn't his only advantage. A gift for spatial reasoning gave him an internal compass to find his way even somewhere he'd never been. He was guided by Naismith's Rule, figured by Scottish mountaineer William W. Naismith before the turn of the century—an able man could cover five kilometers in an hour, with an additional hour allotted for every six hundred meters of ascent.

Though the ground here was hilly, no high peaks waited to interrupt him and his goal; it should take somewhere between twelve minutes and a quarter hour to cover the ground back to the farm. Of course, if Nielsen was just making a drop and then leaving, Sand would be damn well buggered. Once committing to this jungle jaunt, he was giving up at least half an hour by car in each direction.

But who the bloody hell drove two hours out of the city if they weren't going to stay a while?

Fourteen minutes later, from a hill overlooking the streaky white brick farmhouse, Sand's instincts were rewarded—the Mercedes was parked beneath a tree in the bare dirt front yard. Nielsen and his driver were inside, apparently.

But with how many others, and who the hell were they?

Relatively safe in this elevation of underbrush and shadows, finding a fallen tree to provide cover, Sand had an ideal overview of the yard, though of course no idea what was going on inside. To know more, he would have to move closer. But there were stumbling blocks.

The rambling one-story farmhouse was on land carved out of the jungle, a wide open grassy ring setting it off. A few locals and Anglos in straw hats, soiled shirts and jeans milled here and there, two by the crushed-rock driveway, several more at either end of a veranda. None held weapons, but shotguns leaned against a tree near the driveway, and a Schmeisser MP40 lay on a table near the man at this end of the veranda. Sand could only assume the man at the other end was similarly armed.

In the jungle across the yard, motion in the shadows indicated at least one and likely several more roaming guards. He hunkered down lower behind the fallen tree. If he waited till after Nielsen left, and then after nightfall, perhaps he could find out who the ex-Nazi was visiting. That meant letting Nielsen slip away, which might be worth it—if Sand's luck held, perhaps Milan Meier would be in that house.

Hearing movement to his left, Sand turned his head incrementally and picked up a guard coming toward him. He melted back into the shadows, willing his breathing to even itself out, damn near putting himself into a trance, every other living thing in this jungle making more noise and more movement than John Sand.

The guard—tall, with blond hair peeking out beneath an olive drab fatigue hat matching an anonymously military uniform—stopped less than a meter up the hill from Sand, a Schmeisser MP40 hanging by a strap from his shoulder. Looking around, the sentry withdrew a pack of Hollywood brand cigarettes from his shirt pocket, shook one out, and used a lighter.

Sand ticked the seconds off in his head—in two minutes he would have to do something about the guard, and in that event hoped he could do so with a minimum of noise. A minute approached and still the sentry stood looking down the hill at the farmhouse as if there were something interesting about it, smoking his local cigarette, a brand Sand had tried once, and only once. Of the one-hundred-and-twenty seconds Sand had allowed, one hundred had passed when the guard and his nasty cigarette finally continued on his round, moving off to the right.

When the guard rustling through the underbrush was no longer audible, with the smell of that rank cigarette dissipated as well, Sand returned to his fallen tree and again gave his attention to the farmhouse.

And he was just in time—the chauffeur was already in the yard, heading for the Mercedes, with Nielsen coming out the front. The ex-Nazi lingered on the modest veranda as a man in a knee-length white coat and black tie joined him. Nielsen's apparent host had dark hair, clipped close, was rather tall and broad-shouldered, with a friendly gap-toothed smile under a thick dark mustache. The host had a manila envelope under his arm, and seemed jovial, and yet...something arrogant clung to him, something at once regal and distasteful.

And with sudden absolute clarity, Sand recognized Nielsen's host.

The Todesengel.

The Angel of Death.

The demonic Nazi doctor from Auschwitz whose heinous experiments in the name of "research" maimed and butchered hundreds before they were sent to the gas chambers.

Sand had never seen Josef Mengele in the flesh, but that was who this was, all right.

His grip tightening around the Walther, Sand had to stop himself from rushing down this hillside and putting two rounds in Josef Mengele's evil goddamn skull before shooting anyone who had a contrary opinion. The beast responsible for so much death, so much suffering, needed putting down like the mad dog he was, although the mercy of that was itself sickening. For a man who had dispensed more than his own share of death, John Sand was not one to revel in murder—but he would bask in the spilled blood of this Nazi.

So rapt was he in his hunger to murder the murderer of so many, John Sand did not hear the guard approaching from the far end of his stroll.

"*Was ist das?*" the guard said quietly, the Schmeisser pointed casually at Sand.

Grabbing his leg, Sand said, "*Wanderung! Ich bin gefallen, ich glaube ich habe mir den Knöchel gebrochen.*"

Hiking! I've fallen, I think I broke my ankle.

The ploy worked just long enough for the guard to take two steps closer to the writhing stranger, who kicked out, sweeping the man's legs out from under him, sending the sentry tumbling onto his backside. Sand leapt onto him like a panther, punched him in the face, twice, hard, breaking the man's nose and shattering front teeth, then used the strap of the Schmeisser around his neck; strangling him took several minutes, uncomfortable minutes for both.

Hovering over the limp figure, Sand hoped he hadn't taken his rage against Mengele out on this poor bastard. He supposed he could have gone for a quicker, less brutal kill. On the other hand, dead was dead.

Down below, Nielsen was being ushered in back of the Mercedes, with Mengele tossing a wave and ducking back into the house. Other sentries, who'd apparently heard their now deceased comrade calling out to Sand, were on the move, spotting their prey, bringing their weapons up, and shouting in German.

Killing Mengele would have to wait for another day.

Key thing now was getting out of here and back to the Ford, which Sand knew was waiting for him and they didn't. He took off in a straight line through the jungle, its thickness making way for him, though its leaves and fronds filed their objections in more than triplicate, cutting his face and hands as he sprinted; but he had enough of a lead to outrun the men, though of course he wouldn't be able to outrun their bullets.

So after he'd sprinted that hundred meters—with the guards coming up behind him, one stopping to check on their fallen comrade, another firing wildly, his Schmeisser chewing up swinging palm fronds that their quarry was already well past—Sand peeled off and tucked behind a nice plump tree, even as the first shots of his pursuers echoed and scared the wildlife, evidenced by the flutter of wings and scurry of small feet.

His pursuers may have been decent guards, but as a hunting party they were woefully unprepared. The three grouped together, a fourth man trailing well behind after checking on the dead guard.

As they came into range, Sand—not even breathing hard now, the tree concealing him well—peered around and took careful aim. Two went down with a single shot each and the third had sense to throw himself on the jungle floor.

When that man went down, Sand took off toward his car again, resuming his straight line. For a while not a sound came from the remaining two and he wondered if they'd given up the hunt. Then the crackling of a Schmeisser behind him said otherwise.

The bullets were nowhere near him. The Schmeisser, Sand well knew, was an efficient enough weapon, but really only accurate to about seventy meters at most. And that was when the man firing it wasn't running through a jungle.

Finding a shadowy spot, Sand ducked in and crouched and waited. The last two guards came running past, slowing down when they realized they couldn't see him, and when they paused, he rose, dispensing head shots to each. Ribbons of red celebrated his victory as they fell into the tall grass.

After sprinting the rest of the way back to his car, Sand got in, fired it up, and took off back to São Paulo, gliding past Mengele's farm without a glance.

He could use a shower and a meal and some decent sleep. Calling Lyman to brief the CIA agent on these events was all the time he'd allow. The five men he killed would not haunt him before, during, or after his dreams.

They were soldiers, or thought they were, and Nazis, or aspired to such. And they'd worked for Josef Mengele.

They could wait in Hell for their employer. He hoped it wouldn't be long.

* * * * * *

After his speech, Michel Hearn had taken no questions, exiting the way he'd entered—through a door that Stacey and Charlotte, when they found their way to it, found locked.

The rest of the day and that evening they'd stayed on the alert for Michel Hearn, attending panels, lectures and various events where he would seem a logical attendee—without success. A call from a local GUILE rep to Cointrin, home of Geneva's airport, confirmed Hearn had left early in the afternoon on a flight to Buenos Aires, hardly unusual for an Argentinian citizen.

That had been three days ago. After the conference, Stacey and Charlotte flew from Geneva to Las Vegas where Lord Marbury informed them they'd be sent together to Buenos Aires to continue efforts to find Hearn and ascertain his intentions. Double M also reported on John's Sâo Paulo assignment.

"Petrus is confirmed as ex-SS officer Johan Nielsen," Double M said, then added, as if a minor footnote, "who appears to be aligned with Josef Mengele, currently living on a Brazilian farm."

The two women, seated opposite Marbury behind his massive desk in the near replica of his MI6 office, goggled at each other.

"Well," Stacey said, still wide-eyed as she addressed their superior, "that would seem a significant discovery."

Double M granted her a small shrug. "Your husband has always been a capable agent."

Leaning forward, Charlotte said, "So this Meier—he is mixed up with these Nazis in South America? To what end? Are they not busy evading justice for their war crimes?"

"Interesting questions, Agent DuBois," Double M said. "The answers to which may be waiting for you ladies in Buenos Aires. Lovely there this time of year."

Now, twenty-four hours later in Buenos Aires, the "ladies" sat on opposite sides of a table in a muggy, claustrophobic room in the Hall of Civil Registration. Massive leather-bound volumes were piled everywhere, each marked on the spine with a capital H. They were poring over birth records going as far back as 1925 and up to 1937.

Pointing to a line written in fountain pen decades ago, Charlotte said, "Here is what we seek, *mon chéri*. Michel Hearn was born on the second of December 1934. And here is something even more interesting."

"What would that be?"

"Michel Hearn, he dies on the third. *Pauvre bébé*, he live only one day."

Stacy frowned. "Could this be the wrong Michel Hearn?"

"Normally I would say that is possible. But we have spent five hours, going through how many volumes of births that begin with the letter H. How many Hearns have *you* discovered?"

"Not one," Stacey said.

"And this is my first. A German surname among so many Herreras, Hernandezes, and Hidalgos, it should be an apple among oranges, no?"

"Yes."

Charlotte slapped the page in the big book. "Yet we have not found a single other one—only this perfect match. What does that tell you?"

"That the man calling himself Michel Hearn is using the name of a long dead child."

Nodding, Charlotte said, "And this false Michel Hearn is who you suspect him to be."

Stacey had shared her gut feeling that Hearn was Milan Meier.

"Just because a child of that name died," Stacey said, "doesn't prove this false Hearn is the real Meier—there are considerable physical differences."

Charlotte tossed a hand. "I do not agree. His hair, dyed. He puts on the pounds, perhaps purposely. His eyes, they hide behind dark lenses. He lowers his speaking voice. A deception *élémentaire*."

"But his features are slightly...off."

"Plastic surgery," Charlotte said with a shrug.

Stacey frowned. "Did you see any scars, any sign that work had been done?"

"We did not get close enough to detect that, did we? Anyway, such scars are tucked in the folds of existing flesh. And there are rumors of exceptional surgery that avoid the tight look of the facelift, which can change features more radically than ever thought possible.... This is just talk, I admit—never making it into intelligence reports from any of the Global Unit's affiliated countries."

"Would they report something like that?"

"*Oh mon Dieu, oui!* Plastic surgery so expert it could render a person unidentifiable and leave little or no trace, after healing? What the enemies of the Free World might do with such a weapon! The mind, it boggles."

"You consider plastic surgery a weapon?"

She threw up her hands. "It's not just a *Meier* changing into a *Hearn*—what if a double were substituted for President De Gaulle or your Kennedy? Assassinate and replace! Military coups secretly staged! What wickedness might ensue on the world stage?"

The melodrama of Charlotte's rant almost made Stacey smile.

Almost.

"That might be just one of any number of things," Stacey admitted, "that Milan Meier might wish to discuss with Josef Mengele."

CHAPTER FIVE
"ICH BIN EIN BERLINER!"

John Sand's former colleague–the now bestselling author who had fictionalized Sand's adventures into books that were becoming enormously successful films—had once pointed out that Berlin smelled of cigars and boiled cabbage.

This observation, Sand had to admit, wasn't entirely without merit. Of course, it was perhaps the nicest thing his friend had said about a city and its people, who lived in what was now the divided former capital of Germany. The writer hadn't really liked the place even before that country itself was split in two after the Second World War.

Sand's own thoughts were slightly kinder—slightly. They were colored to a degree by his last visit, in '59, when he had been kidnapped, hidden away in the *Führerbunker* tunnels below the city. A hired assassin had left him in the care of four German gunmen with instructions to torture and murder him. This tended to blot out any of the fonder memories Sand might have about Berlin.

Yet here he was again, sent on a chartered plane by Double M and whisked into this small side office in the *Rathaus Schöneberg*, West Berlin's City Hall, without even time to change into a fresh Savile Row suit. The room was uncomfortably warm, windows closed, curtains drawn against the summer sun. A Tensor lamp and an ashtray perched on a small table with two straight-back wooden chairs, much like the one to which he had been tied on his previous visit.

Shrugging to himself, he settled into a chair. This tableau reminded him far too much of his visit to those tunnels, lacking only the assassin as host with those four German gunmen in attendance. When the doorknob twisted, he almost expected hired guns to step in.

In a way he was right, but these two gunslingers were members of the US Secret Service, their dark suits and ties almost similar enough to qualify as uniforms. Both wore sunglasses, which they left on despite the sun remaining outdoors to wait for them.

The blond one nodded to him, and the redheaded one said, "Always a pleasure, sir."

"We have to quit meeting like this," Sand said, and stood, holding his arms out and up, to allow patting down by the redhead, who asked, "The usual ordinance?"

Walther in shoulder rig, Beretta in ankle holster.

"Take them if you like," Sand said.

The red-headed agent said, "We have instructions not to. But under these conditions, we do have to check."

"Understood. Thank you for the courtesy."

The blond agent knocked twice on the closed door, paused, then knocked once more.

Moments later, sweeping in and removing his own dark glasses, came President John F. Kennedy. His reddish-brown hair was parted to one side, his black suit crisply immaculate, his shirt a blinding white, his eyes a greenish-gray with a sparkle even in the meager cast of the desk lamp.

Sand, still on his feet, was not easily intimidated or impressed; but having this famous figure smiling big and thrusting out a hand to shake had its surreal aspect.

"John," Kennedy said, his smile lingering at the edge of one cheek. "How the hell are you?"

"Somewhat the hell *surprised*, sir, actually."

Kennedy gripped the agent's shoulder and squeezed in a friendly way. "Surely you recognized this pair of shadows of mine."

Kennedy nodded to them, and the two Secret Service agents smiled, nodded, and slipped out the door through which he'd entered, closing the other two men in.

Sand said, "Oh, I figured where your shadows preceded, you would follow. But I've only had a minute or two to consider that—no one told me we'd be meeting. And I'm in Berlin on what I thought was an unrelated matter."

The hand-on-shoulder came away, the smile too, replaced by a business-like nod.

"Precisely why," the President of the United States said, "I thought we should talk today."

Kennedy gestured for Sand to resume his chair and pulled the other around to face the agent. As had become a ritual on their meetings, the President withdrew two cigars from the inside breast pocket of his suitcoat. His expression turned oddly wistful as he handed the smoke to Sand.

"H. Upmann Petit Coronas," Kennedy said.

"Your favorite, sir...and mine. The finest Cuban tobacco."

"And the, uh, last two I *have*, John."

"More's the pity, Mr. President. Embargoes do take their toll on both sides."

Kennedy nodded. "That we are sharing my last pair of

these valuable items should tell you this meeting is not a social one, because we, uh, both just happen to be in the city at the same time."

The President used a small cigar cutter, which he handed over to Sand, and then the process was reversed. They took turns using Sand's lighter to get their cigars going. For a few moments, they sat smoking in silence, enjoying the precious Cuban exports.

Finally, the President said, as casually as if their discussion of tobacco might be continuing, "Some of Dulles's people over at CIA think your friend Meier is trying to get enough uranium to build an atomic bomb."

Sand sucked in smoke, held it, let it out. "That Meier is a 'friend' is obvious sarcasm. As for acquiring enough uranium to build himself a bomb? I would say your characterization is unfortunately accurate."

"John, as the one who's looking for him, do you think Meier may have achieved that goal?"

Sand nodded slowly. "I would say he already has enough to build himself not just a bomb, but something of a nuclear arsenal."

Kennedy frowned. This clearly was even worse news than he thought he might get from the operative.

Sand plowed on. "With what his cronies smuggled out of the Kazakh Soviet Socialist Republic, Meier has enough uranium to become the equivalent of a nuclear power. Less so than the USA or the USSR, of course...a power nonetheless."

"Does he have the technology to develop such weapons?"

"He might, sir."

Kennedy frowned. "Would you care to explain that? Are you talking about him getting help from the Soviets?"

"Worse," Sand said.

The rather hooded eyes opened wide. "What's worse than the goddamn Soviets?"

"The goddamn Nazis."

Kennedy lifted his chin, narrowed his eyes—had he misheard? "You're flashing back a war there, aren't you, John? *Nazis?* And even if they were, uh, still a threat, whatever ragtag rabble remains of them...where would they access nuclear scientists?"

Sand let some cigar smoke trail out as he calmly said, "The same way you Americans did. Do I need to say more than Operation Paperclip?"

After the war, the United States government had brought over sixteen-hundred Nazi V-2 scientists to work with NASA.

"Lord Marbury has briefed me, of course," Kennedy said off-handedly, "about what you encountered in Brazil. And I'm encouraged that we finally have a bead on Mengele."

Sand grimaced. "I'm afraid *I* had a bead on the bastard and didn't take the shot."

Kennedy waved that off. "I'm sure you would have, had the circumstances allowed. In the meantime, we've shared that intel with GUILE's Mossad members. Has there been progress on the Mengele front?"

Sand shook his head. "Global Unit agents went to raid that farmhouse and found it empty, stripped even of furnishings. People in the area were questioned and knew nothing of their neighbor except his reclusive nature. No one employed by him was identified. The dead had been carted off."

Kennedy frowned, his upper lip twitching. "So the Angel of Death has slipped through our fingers."

"Yes, sir. And I have to take some responsibility for that."

"Nonsense." He gestured with cigar in hand. "Where are we with Milan Meier?"

"My wife and another agent are in Argentina, tracking him through a borrowed identity he's assumed. They're on his trail, Mr. President."

Kennedy knocked ash off his cigar into a tray on the nearby table. "How many Nazis in Argentina, John?"

"Several thousand, sir. Probably over ten thousand in South America. More than a 'ragtag' group, I'm afraid, if a leader can bring them together."

The greenish-blue eyes narrowed. "Do you think Meier is that leader?"

"Possibly. Or he may be a stalking horse. Every Jesus needs a John the Baptist."

A wry smile came to the famous lips. "Let's not compare the Nazis to Christians, John."

"Well, that's what they thought they were. *Think* they are, I should say."

Kennedy shuddered. "Disconcerting to be discussing an extension of the last war when we so recently avoided the next one. Can the world be on fire again so soon?"

That was obviously a rhetorical question, but Sand answered it: "In my experience, sir, the world is on fire most of the time."

Kennedy sighed. "My opinion, as well, I'm afraid. But I just dealt with Khrushchev and Castro and that goddamned missile mess. How about you and Lord Marbury take care of this one? If you can confirm the atomic threat, and specifically tie it to a resurgence of these Nazi sons of bitches, I'll bring whatever firepower you need in off the bench. What do you say?"

Sand knew mentioning the Bay of Pigs would be an impropriety, and decided to take the promise at face value.

"Well, I say...yes, sir."

Another smile, but business-like. "What does Marbury have in mind for you next, John? Joining your wife in Argentina, I would think."

"As soon as I leave here, Mr. President."

Kennedy got to his feet. The two men exchanged warm smiles and tight handshakes, Kennedy saying, "Don't let me keep you, John. And I, uh, have a speech to make."

His manner pleasant but the meeting clearly over, the leader of the Free World went over and knocked on the door, twice and a pause and another knock, and the two Secret Service agents collected Sand and led him around through heavy security to a rear exit. Like the President, Sand held onto his cigar. He would smoke his as long as possible, and he imagined the same was true of his friend, the President.

Sand was well-aware that three-hundred-thousand-some Berliners were waiting for the leader of the Free World to inspire them. At the rear only a few people were milling, primarily German security guards and assorted Secret Service agents; but Sand might well have been in the midst of the throng on the other side of the massive stone building, fired up by Konrad Adenauer, the chancellor's amplified voice receiving nearly constant applause.

Sand walked to the corner of the building hoping to find an easy path to a street where he might hail a taxi for a ride back to the airport. Here he found the crowd only thicker and more ebullient. This far back it would be hard to see their celebrated visitor, but they would hear him.

Slowly, Sand worked his way between the excited Berliners. Off to the right was an apartment building, and if he could just get there, perhaps he could sneak through and come out on the other side out of the human tide. His goal was a six-story rectangle, its narrow end facing the crowd, City Hall and the adjacent stage—two windows on each floor, some open, people all but hanging out of them for a better view of the President, who Adenauer was introducing even now.

Then, above the windows, on the building's flat roof, a small pipe caught Sand's attention. He used his hand to shade his eyes, but he knew at once what it was he was looking at.

A rifle barrel.

Damn!

Adenauer's voice, amplified, said, "*President John F. Kennedy!*"

The crowd erupted around Sand as if they'd just been told that the *verdammt* wall was coming down—the noise engulfed him, as did citizens jumping up and down and waving flags of both nations and jostling back and forth as if in gleeful battle. Suddenly moving through this undulating mass became almost impossible.

No time to alert anyone, no returning to the Secret Service agents in the back of City Hall—only one thing to do: plow ahead or be damned.

From the stage, Kennedy's amplified voice was saying, "*I am proud to come to this city as the guest of your distinguished mayor who has symbolized throughout the world, the fighting spirit of West Berlin.*"

Sand had just been gaining some momentum getting through the crowd when the mention of the mayor and West Berlin caused applause to erupt again, freezing him until they calmed slightly, their own movement stilled as they were swept up in the charismatic presence of this visitor.

Then Sand was again swimming upstream, fighting a choppy current, like the last remaining salmon determined to keep his species alive.

"*And I am proud to visit the Federal Republic with your distinguished chancellor who for so many years has committed Germany to democracy and freedom and progress.*"

He was making better progress now, too, though those he bumped and slipped between were swearing at him, in colorful German mostly, as he pushed his way through, glancing up now and then at a rifle barrel still sticking off the edge of the roof.

"*And to come here in the company of my fellow American General Clay...*"

Up ahead, the doors of the building called to him, as Kennedy mentioned General Lucius Clay, the American senior officer in charge of administering the governorship of Berlin, who personally ordered the Berlin Airlift before President Truman okayed it to overcome the Berlin Blockade.

This prompted the crowd to again explode in applause and cheers, pushing Sand back, until he managed to hold his ground and continue forward again, pushing past and between people, the barrel of the gun seen by no one else but him, taunting him as if only he noticed the Emperor's lack of clothes.

No longer listening to Kennedy, ignoring the crowd's occasional eruptions into applause, Sand focused only on moving forward and as fast as he could manage, as much as he might dare. He of course considered drawing his pistol, but that would be the last resort in a crowd this size, risking being swarmed and drawing attention but not to the unseen gun threatening their guest, even providing a shooter with a distraction that would only aid assassination.

Kennedy said, "*Two thousand years ago the proudest boast was* 'civis Romanus sum.' *Today, in the world of freedom, the proudest boast is* 'Ich bin ein Berliner.'"

Once more, the multitude burst into applause, but this time instead of surging forward, this flank of the crowd parted. Sand rushed through the sudden open hole, getting within a few meters of the apartment house door before the crowd closed up that opening.

He fought through the remaining people with relative ease. The building's doors stood open and Sand rushed in. The lobby and corridors of this venerable apartment house with its dark woodwork, two-tone walls and tile flooring were as empty as the street outside was packed. Not even bothering with the lift, Sand pulled his Walther and sprinted up the stairs from floor to floor, pausing only occasionally to see if the sniper had a cohort posted.

On the last step before the top floor, Sand peeked around the corner and saw a big blond man standing sentry at what must be the door to the roof. A gunshot would warn the sniper of company, and while that might have scared the shooter, it might also propel him into immediate action. He didn't need the gunman getting an itchier trigger finger than he might already have.

At the same time, Sand was puzzled by the sniper not having fired by now. What was the hell was he waiting for? But this was no time to be anything but grateful for that small favor. Slipping the Walther back under his left arm, but leaving his suitcoat unbuttoned, Sand sauntered onto the floor as if he was lost.

With an awkward smile, Sand asked, "*Männerzimmer?*"
Men's room?

The guard snapped at him, "*Verpissen!*"
Fuck off!

Sand winced in apparent confusion and approached the man, saying awkwardly,"*Entschuldigung, ich spreche wenig Deutsch.*"

Sorry, I don't speak much German.

The sentry turned toward him now; he was clutching something, which a *snick* and flash of steel announced as a long sharp blade.

"Don't," Sand advised, but the guard came at him, slashing.

Sand spun, the knife cutting only air as it flew past him before he elbowed the sentry in the face, breaking the man's nose with a brittle crack. As the guard howled, Sand grabbed the man's knife arm, twisting it up, blade pointing to the ceiling now, another twist and the knife clattered to the floor as Sand brought the man's elbow down, bending it the wrong way, breaking the sentry's arm with a crack loud enough to echo in the corridor, and dropping him to his knees where Sand took him by the head and broke his neck with a louder crack still, a move not easily performed but long since perfected by the agent.

Sand collected the switchblade, leaving its blade open and ready.

He threw the roof door open and sunlight came down a short steep flight of stairs, the door at the other end propped open. He went up two at a time, knife in hand, then peeked out, the sniper prone on the roof, just another working man in coveralls...looking through a rifle's telescopic sight.

The crack of a gunshot, whether his or the sniper's, would send the crowd into a panicked frenzy and get people trampled. If that shot were the sniper's, it might take the life of the President of the United States, a man Sand had come to consider a friend.

Stepping out onto the flat roof—the throng clearly visible beyond the lip of the building, the stage and its podium and speaker too—Sand rejected of the option of creeping up to the sniper without giving himself away. And with the sun behind him, he'd cast a shadow that would fall on the killer before he could jump the bastard.

The agent took one step and flung the knife, sending it tumbling end over end, on a deadly path that seemed to take forever. When it struck home, the sniper grunted and arched his back and turned toward the pain with an expression of surprise and dismay. The rifle slipped from his grip onto the roof, barrel still extending over if not as far. An arm jerked spasmodically back as if he might pull the blade out, then the air, the life, went out of him and he fell forward as if sleep had suddenly taken him.

And hadn't it?

As Sand breathed a sigh of relief, Kennedy saying, "*What is true of this city is true of Germany—real, lasting peace in Europe can never be assured as long as one German out of four is denied the elementary right of free men, and that is to make a free choice.*"

Sand went to the dead assassin and withdrew the switchblade from the man's back, wiping the handle of his fingerprints and tossing it.

"*In eighteen years of peace and good faith, this generation of Germans has earned the right to be free, including the right to unite their families and their nation in lasting peace, with good will to all people.*"

He turned the body over.

The dead man—eyes open though expressionless, thinning dark blond hair swept back, skin pale, mustache curving—was Jürgen Becker, hired assassin, expert marksman with a rifle, an ability honed in service to the Fatherland during the Second World War.

Sand would have recognized this killer even without

the Odal rune, a swastika-like symbol tattooed on the back of Becker's left hand, a souvenir of his gory glory days in the SS.

Kennedy's speech continued: "*You live in a defended island of freedom, but your life is part of the main. So let me ask you as I close, to lift your eyes beyond the dangers of today, to the hopes of tomorrow, beyond the freedom merely of this city of Berlin, or your country of Germany, to the advance of freedom everywhere, beyond the wall to the day of peace with justice, beyond yourselves and ourselves to all mankind.*"

The crowd roared approval again as Sand went through Becker's pockets. A new wallet held three hundred *Deutsche* marks—with an exchange rate of nearly four to one, about twelve hundred US dollars. He pocketed the money, ran through the wallet, found nothing else, not even forged ID; then he put it back into Becker's pocket.

The Mauser Karabiner 98K with a ZF39 scope had likely been Becker's only tool of the trade since the *Waffen* SS. Sand wouldn't have minded confiscating the rifle for his own use, but one simply couldn't walk through the streets of Berlin carrying a rifle.

Some things just were not done.

And if he couldn't carry a rifle through the streets of Berlin today, neither could Becker. Which meant someone in the middle of the night had dropped Becker off with his rifle and spotter, or they had been staying in this apartment house before the speech.

Kennedy's visit was no state secret—anything but. Every in Berlin would have figured he'd speak, and once the bunting started going up at the *Rathaus Schöneberg*, knowing where that would take place required no great military acumen.

Back downstairs to the sixth floor, Sand rifled the dead sentry's pockets, finding a few D-Marks, but nothing else of interest. This dead man was younger than the one on the roof, an apprentice perhaps. Walking along the corridor, Sand tried doorknobs. Each was locked. But nearing the fallen man, one door was unlocked.

Sand stepped inside. The furniture was old and bland. No family pictures rode the walls or were propped on tables; nothing personal presented itself anywhere in the shabby living room or kitchen. Clothing in drawers was old, often frayed, with not even a laundry mark. A number printed on a disc in the center of the telephone dial he memorized.

In one of two bedrooms, he found a board removed from the floor beneath the sagging bed. Becker's plan was to apparently shoot Kennedy, come downstairs, enter the apartment, hide the rifle in the floor, then either slip way or simply hide in plain sight when the *Berliner Polizei* searched the building.

Returning to the living room, Sand called GUILE HQ in Berlin and requested cleanup. He didn't know the address, so he simply described the building, then asked for checks on the name on the lease and the phone records for the last week from that apartment. Satisfied, he hung up and this time took the lift down.

Outside, looking past the crowd toward the podium, he could barely identify the figure of Kennedy from this distance, though the President's amplified voice carried just fine.

Allowing himself a smile at the thought of what he'd just prevented, Sand pondered why he seemed to be running into Nazis at every turn. He needed to get to Argentina and join up with Stacey and Charlotte. Perhaps the three of them could put this damn thing together.

Kennedy said, "*All free men, wherever they may live, are citizens of Berlin, and, therefore, as a free man, I take pride in the words* 'Ich bin ein Berliner.'"

Sand paused to join in the applause.

TWO

PILGRIM'S PROGRESS
JULY-NOVEMBER 1963

CHAPTER SIX

DON'T SPY FOR ME, ARGENTINA

Though July was the dead of winter in Buenos Aires, Sand landed at Aeroparque Jorge Newbery to find the temperature in the pleasant fifties. He didn't need a topcoat over his gray Savile suitcoat; and unlike many who wore such expensive threads, he did not don a tie, although he did accessorize with the Walther P38, for which his tailor had compensated more than adequately.

Stacey and Charlotte were there to meet him, which gave him both a thrill and a spot of trepidation—the notion of the two women who'd been the most important in his life (and not just his love life) rubbing shoulders and presumably talking about him, well, it was troubling. But there they were, all smiles and standing close enough to... rub shoulders.

As usual, Stacey looked smashing in her black Givenchy dress under its lightweight matching coat, her auburn hair swept back into a ponytail against the Argentine breeze. Likewise, Charlotte was simply stunning, her dark hair tied back, her lime coat over a floral green-yellow-pink pants suit.

As soon as he was down the stairs and onto the tarmac, Stacey was in his arms; they kissed as if he'd just come back from some war or other, and that wasn't far wrong. Past her wide-eyed gaze he discreetly took in Charlotte standing with arms folded and lips pursed in an enigmatic smile.

Stacey was saying, "I want to hear all about it!"

They broke from their embrace and strolled hand in hand to Charlotte. "All about what?"

"Germany, you big ape! What in God's name happened there?"

"Nothing at all to do with God, actually." He nodded to Charlotte, who had fallen in on the other side of him as they walked. "How did you hear anything of note happened there?"

Though that had been addressed to his wife, it was Charlotte who answered: "Double M explained your delay by saying you had to be...debriefed."

Charlotte could make "debriefed" sound so very sensual.

But she was right about his delay. Delivered by phone, on a secure line but nonetheless in an elliptical fashion, the broad strokes of Sand stopping that rooftop assassin were not enough for Lord Marbury. Sand was directed to return to Las Vegas for a debriefing that had taken the better part of a day and had been anything but sensual. Now he was in for another round of questions that would easily match the intensity of Double M's.

They walked from baggage claim to the nondescript dark-blue Chevrolet sedan GUILE had provided the women. An arm around Stacey's shoulders, Charlotte brushing against him on the other side, Sand told his lovers past and present how he had spotted the rifle barrel on the apartment house roof and "dispatched" both the lookout and the sniper, notorious ex-Nazi assassin, Jürgen Becker.

"It's starting to sound," Stacey said with a shiver, "like there's nothing 'ex' about any of these Nazis."

"You are not wrong, darling," he said.

Charlotte drove, Sand at the passenger window with Stacey between them on the bench-style seat. They were only a kilometer and a half from downtown.

The driver said, a weary bitterness in her voice, "Does it never end?"

Sand knew what she meant, but Stacey asked, "Does what never end?"

"The *putain de* Nazis! I have been fighting them since the day I join *Le Résistance*."

"You were in the Resistance?" Stacey asked, obviously impressed. "You must have been a child."

When Charlotte and Sand were colleagues years ago, the former *Service de Documentation Extérieure et Contre-Espionage* (SDECE) operative had rarely spoken of those days—it took something special to stir up those memories.

Nazis would do it.

Eyes on the busy city street, Charlotte said, "I *was* a child, I suppose. Thirteen? Doing reconnaissance. When the Boche capture a young girl, they would violate her, passing her around like *un bouteille de bière* before killing her. I learned to be a invisible, slip unseen from here to there...and to sleep with both eyes open, *n'est pas?*"

Stacey clutched Sand's hand.

Her voice steady, detached, Charlotte said, "I killed my first German soldier three days after my fourteenth birthday. With his own gun. His pants around his ankles, about my older brother's age—twenty?" She shrugged, as if recalling her first day at school. "I have been fighting

Nazis for most of my life. And now I fight them again."

Silence followed, Stacey clearly feeling awkward by what Charlotte had shared with such sudden frankness. Sand had heard it all before, though not often, and the horror resurfacing now spoke volumes.

He said, casually, "We don't know yet what we're up against. I'm happy to root out a few war criminals if the opportunity presents itself. But before we assume a new Third...or would that be Fourth?...Reich is assembling itself, let's find out what the estimable Milan Meier is up to. I hate it when rich men make collecting uranium their hobby."

But Sand knew a few words of reason from him were unlikely to harness Charlotte's ghosts. He had his own specters and knew damn well that keeping them in check was no small task.

"Here we are," Charlotte said, pulling into a small parking lot adjacent to a squat office building that appeared to consist of old bricks and the memory of mortar.

"I hope this is not," Sand said, "our hotel."

"This," Stacey said, "is GUILE's local HQ—not quite the Destiny in Vegas."

"But our destiny in Buenos Aires," he said.

"Yes, and it's been our home away from home while Charlotte and I have been plowing through records."

This unprepossessing HQ was a few blocks from downtown in an out-of-the-way neighborhood swarming with secondary professional buildings filled with insurance agencies, doctors' offices, and accountancies. This nondescript pile of bricks bore a small brass sign that in gold letters on black read GLOBAL UNITED LTD., a designation as accurate as it was nebulous.

Sand held the glass door open for the women and the

trio entered a small empty lobby—speckled marble floor, plaster walls, minus even one chair or solitary potted palm. At the lone elevator, Charlotte inserted into a camlock a small key, which (in an echo of Vegas procedure) she turned. The elevator doors groaned open, as if irritated.

A modern keypad within a venerable elevator car required Stacey entering a code, and one floor up the doors opened onto another glass-box cubicle like the one at the Destiny; this bullet-proof box contained a young Hispanic male at a metal desk with a few magazines (*Manchete, O Cruzeiro*), half a *Bauru* sandwich and a thermos. He wore a navy-blue suit, his black hair slicked and parted, his smile friendly—he obviously recognized the two women—although of course Sand was a stranger, which may have been why the young man's right hand remained under the desk, almost certainly holding a pistol.

"Mrs. Sand," he said pleasantly. "Miss DuBois."

"This is Mr. Sand, Jaime," Stacey said. "As expected."

Sand followed Stacey and Charlotte to a metallic sliding door next to which was a TV-style screen, semi-circular red and green lights above it, unlit at the moment.

Each in turn pressed palms to the screen, a light above flaring green. The door buzzed open and they entered a short conical metal-lined hallway not unlike one at the former GUILE headquarters in the Vegas neon graveyard. Another metal door waited, a camera over it.

This time Charlotte punched a numbered code into a keyboard next to the door.

Sand asked, "No one to open it from the inside?"

Stacey said, "No one here but us spies."

He frowned, threw a thumb over his shoulder. "Just us and that boy?"

Charlotte said, "That 'boy,' he is a sharpshooter and

hand-to-hand combat expert, old enough to have served with distinction in *Exército Brasileiro.*"

The land arm of the Brazilian Armed Forces.

As they walked into the inner office, Charlotte flipped a light switch. Four desks, two piled with papers, the other two with telephones, were about the extent of it, with the exception of a small refrigerator and one of those big bulky gray photocopying machines, crouched against the wall like a slumbering beast. Sand and Stacey pulled two chairs over around one desk, piled with the photocopies.

Seating herself behind that desk, Charlotte said, "Only four agents work out of here, two per shift. And those two, right now, are out doing legwork for us."

Stacey said, "We're our own office staff for now."

Sand nodded. "What have you found?"

"Michel Hearn is Milan Meier, all right," Stacey said, "but his appearance somewhat belies that. I frankly couldn't tell for certain it was him."

"How close did you get to the man?"

"Not close enough," she admitted. "We sat toward the back because we thought Hearn might be there and wanted the whole audience to choose from. We had no idea he'd be the speaker—all we had was a topic on the agenda, something on atomic energy's benefits, which seemed like he'd attend."

Charlotte said, "We tried to catch up to him after, and got closer, which we did. But he slip out a side door...and lock it behind him."

Stacey picked up: "He was heavier than when he called himself Meier, his eyes hidden by tinted glasses, his hair darker, and, yes, both are easily explainable, but his voice was different, and he actually looked...younger."

"Plastic surgery?"

Charlotte said, "That would seem the obvious an-swer, but none of plastic surgery's look of the telltale tightened skin."

Sand frowned. "Any visible scars?"

Stacey said, "No apparent ones—granted, we were only close for a few moments, but by that time I suspected who Hearn really was and was looking. Maybe if I had seen those icy eyes of his behind the dark glasses..."

Sand said, "Contact lenses get around that easily enough."

Like the blue-eyed Kyla Fluss could easily be the brown-eyed Michelle Rivers.

Stacey was saying, "And it wasn't just his voice that was different—he didn't sound Dutch, more...Argentinian."

As perhaps Kyla's German accent had suddenly flown south when she became Michelle Rivers...

"But *what* he said," Stacey went on, "echoed exactly his words in Curaçao...John, are you listening?"

Charlotte said, "You seem somewhere else, *mon ami.*"

"I'm afraid I *was* somewhere else for a moment," he admitted. "São Paulo."

He told them briefly about running into a woman he strongly suspected was a revised edition of Kyla Fluss—the same differences the two women had noticed about Hearn/Meier—hair, weight, accent—paralleling those of Rivers/Fluss.

"And she bumped into me," he said, "at just the right time to keep me from tracking my quarry."

Stacey asked, "John, what the hell is going on?"

"Damned if I know. Let's get back to what you've found out about Hearn."

They filled him in on the identity Meier had stolen from a child born and died in 1934.

Stacey said, "There are no Hearns in the records until

Michel turns up again in July of last year—just a few weeks after Meier escaped from Curaçao."

Sand nodded. "Have you turned up any immigration record of Meier entering the country?"

"No," Stacey said. "He simply vanished—like all of the art and furnishings in his Curaçao mansion."

Charlotte shuffled through some of the photocopies, saying, "We contacted GUILE agents in the Netherlands. Meier's birth certificate there is forgery."

Sand asked, "Have we tracked down his real records yet?"

Shaking her head, Stacey said, "'Milan Meier' is a fabricated identity, although admittedly extremely well contrived."

Holding up two photocopies, Charlotte said, "As well contrived as *this* faux identity..."

She handed both sheets to Sand, who studied them—a birth record for Michel Hearn with no death date; and an approved passport form in the same name.

"These look *légitime*," Charlotte said. "Someone high up had to approve of this, *no*?"

The authorization signature on each document had been signed by a Victor Von Koerber, Minister of Records.

Frowning, Sand asked, "Who is this Von Koerber?"

Both women shook their heads and shrugged.

Sand went over to a phone, thumbed through a directory, then dialed a number. His call was answered on the third ring and, after the receptionist said he had reached the British Embassy and where might she direct his call, Sand said, "Sir Geoffrey Northam, please."

"The ambassador has a most busy schedule, sir, but if you will leave your—"

"Miss, I know Geoffrey is a busy fellow, but if you

would please tell him it's Sand? John Sand? I am quite sure, though you do sound charming, that we could save each other some time by not doing this dance."

Stacey made a face and Charlotte made one back at her.

"Yes, sir, if you'll hold, please."

She clicked off and Sand glanced down at the signatures again.

Then his dancing partner returned: "I'll put you right through, sir. Sorry for your wait."

"Not at all," Sand said.

A deep, rich baritone came on the line. "John, you bloody bastard, is that really you?"

"Mr. Ambassador," Sand said, seeing his old friend in his mind—tall, thin, pale, Northam had always appeared sickly but was anything but. An inveterate long distance runner, and a member of the diplomatic service throughout an active adult life, Northam had attended Eton with Sand.

"Stuff the title, John. What do you need? You've never been terribly social."

"Well, I might be calling just to see how you've been."

"Really? How nice. I have nothing to complain about. Second wife taking nicely. Children of the other wife grown and on their own. Nothing to complain about even if I could find someone to listen, and you surely aren't volunteering."

"Let's just say I didn't call *only* to catch up with an old friend."

"What do you need with a lowly British subject now that you're a rich American with a far younger, more beautiful wife than a scoundrel like you deserves? Are the streets in the States really paved with gold?"

"No. Oil. But it's slippery. And I'm closer to you currently than Texas."

"Interesting. How close?"

"I may be able to introduce you to my lovely wife over dinner this week. But first I have work to do. I need some information."

A pause—brief, but a pause. "We might be getting into a touchy area, John. I serve the Queen, as you may recall. Perhaps you should try the American Embassy."

"If I have to bother Lord Marbury, it could take longer, and I assure you this has nothing to do with the Queen—it's about an Argentinian, who I'm hoping you know."

This pause was more extended, but finally Northam said, "Who might that be?"

"Victor Von Koerber."

"I know the name, John." No pause at all this time. "But I've never met the man."

"Is there anything you might tell me about him?"

A shrug was in the Ambassador's voice as he said, "Von Koerber's in his late fifties, a minister of Records or Transportation or some such—politics here move faster than I can keep up. He had a certain importance when Peron was in power, but since the overthrow in '55, this Von Koerber is something of a recluse. Seldom in Buenos Aires. Has an estate called Inalco House."

Sand was jotting that down on a notepad by the phone. "Inalco House? Where exactly?"

"On the coast of Lake Nahuel Huapi, near the Chilean border."

"If he were to stay in Buenos Aires, visiting or perhaps at a second home or apartment, where might that be?"

The pause that followed was the longest yet, while the ambassador decided what was cricket and what was not. Then: "He has an apartment overlooking the ocean. Doesn't use it much."

Sand felt like he was shucking a peapod, getting one pea at a time.

"You wouldn't happen to know the address, would you?"

"John, you're asking a lot. I work every day to build a sense of trust. The Argentine government are our friends now."

"You would think an old friend of *mine* would save me the trouble of scouting out one miserable address."

Northam growled and rattled off the numbers.

"I owe you, Geoffrey."

"I agree. And when your business allows, if you don't meet me for dinner and introduce me to that fetching creature who is your wife, I will instruct my receptionist that I am permanently unavailable to a particular bloody bastard."

"Love you, too."

They hung up.

Putting down the receiver, Sand turned to Stacey and Charlotte. "We have a place to start."

* * * * * *

For the next two weeks, the trio took shifts watching the apart-ment house—Charlotte overnight, Sand morning through late afternoon, Stacey on through till midnight. This allowed Sand to breakfast with Stacey and sup with Charlotte, with the two women sharing lunch, an arrangement that allowed some reasonable human contact among the little group, albeit requiring discipline on Sand's part, as Charlotte and Stacey seemed to have an unspoken difference in opinion about the sanctity of marriage.

The team varied its approach. From a building across the way, in a rented office suite, they watched through binoculars. Sometimes they would use the Chevrolet, other times a park bench down the block, even a boat in the bay. They were careful, they were meticulous, they were stealthy, but what good did it do? Von Koerber simply was not there. Sand considered shifting to the subject's estate, where they had no reconnaissance to go on, and who knew what might be waiting for them. No other option came to mind.

When Sand turned up for his shift on the morning of the fifteenth day, he found Charlotte sitting in the passenger seat of the Chevrolet, patiently scanning with binoculars the third-floor balcony of the stone apartment building, which each of them had by now pretty well memorized, centimeter by centimeter. The balcony sported a small wrought-iron table and four chairs, leaving little room for anything else. She was sitting up, alert, searching for any sign of movement.

He got in on the driver's side, quietly shut the door, and looked back at her.

"Something?" he asked.

"*Si* ça *se trouve,*" she said.

Perhaps.

"What?" he asked.

"Not long after midnight? A Mercedes limo drops off a man and woman in front. Older couple. Well-dressed. He gives her his arm, yet she seems to be supporting him, as if he is elderly. Three younger, bigger men in dark suits accompany them. Limo drives off, the three younger, bigger men, their eyes are going everywhere."

Bodyguards, he thought.

She was saying, "All five, they go inside. Soon lights in Von Koerber's apartment go on."

Sand nodded slowly. "So he's there."

"This I can only assume. They were little more than silhouettes on the street, and shapes in the windows. Then the lights go off within the hour."

"And they're all still inside?"

She nodded, finally lowering the binoculars. "Our third week, it starts and, finally, we are looking at our man. I hope."

"Good work," he told her. "Grab some breakfast with Stacey at the hotel, and catch some rest."

Charlotte leaned close, bringing her *L'Air du Temps* perfume along for the ride. "She is very sweet, your Stacey, and so kind."

"She is indeed."

"Your attraction to her, I understand. She is very beautiful, intelligent, *dynamique*. But then you always are a lucky man."

Charlotte was close enough to kiss him on the mouth, but instead she chose his cheek before laughing playfully and slipping out of the car. "And she is *très chanceux*, this I know."

A weaker man would have watched her walk away, a female fresh as the morning itself despite her long boring night, that bottom unacquainted with any girdle moving fluidly beneath her skirt; but he looked through his binoculars toward the balcony.

For the next half an hour or so he sat with her perfume clinging like a sleeping lover, his thoughts alternating between memories of two women, then the sliding glass door of Von Koerber's apartment slid open.

Sand sat up.

But nothing happened for several endless moments. Maybe they were just letting in some air.

Finally a tall blond man came out and set the table with plates and silverware. Not a likely butler, in that gray tailored suit similar to Sand's, except this bloke's tailor did not disguise the bulge of the pistol in its shoulder holster nearly as well. The tall blond arranged the two settings next to each other, then went back inside and a second man came out, similar suit, similar under-the-shoulder bulge, carrying a tray with a pitcher of orange juice and two glasses, a carafe of coffee (probably) with two cups, a sugar bowl and cream pitcher, too. Set the beverages down near one chair and the glasses and cups at both.

This was more action than they had seen in the previous fourteen days and nights combined.

The first man returned with a tray of food. From this distance Sand made out eggs but wasn't positive if the meat were bacon or sausage. On the tray was a serving of toast and a butter dish next to a little bowl of something that might be cherry or strawberry jam.

Sand's stomach irritated him by growling. A woman came out onto the balcony, a third armed man in tailored gray guiding her. She was perhaps fifty, a strawberry blonde, maybe fifty-five kilos, in a floral dress with a blue background, a white sweater fighting the morning chill. Something about her seemed familiar, but then she was a type of Germanic beauty he'd encountered often—Kyla Fluss was one; this was an aging flower.

Then the man who had to be Victor Von Koerber strolled out onto the balcony, looking slightly older than the woman, which was about right—Geoffrey had said Von Koerber was in his late fifties. Sand wondered why Charlotte had thought that perhaps the man she saw in the dark last night was elderly.

The apparent Von Koerber did not appear to be Argentinian—not with that pasty face. His dark hair was fairly long, parted on one side and swept over. He wore a smart brown suit, white shirt and a darker brown tie—clean-shaven, several inches under six feet tall, weight about seventy kilos, eyes dark, glittering black in the morning sun, like a shark's. He was smiling, as if he were glad to be alive, and yet somehow he looked unhappy, as if really he were dead.

And it came to Sand: *Could I be looking at...a dead man?*

He lowered the binoculars, blinked slowly, then raised them again. Couldn't be possible—could it? No. No. He *couldn't* be looking at the latter-day face of a clean-shaven madman barely older than he had been when he committed suicide in the *Fuhrerbunker* in 1945.

Adolf Hitler was long dead.

Wasn't he?

CHAPTER SEVEN

MR. SHOWMANSHIP

"Really?" Stacey asked. "'How is breakfast? By the way, Victor Von Koerber would appear to be Adolf Hitler'...?"

Sand's wife and Charlotte were seated at a table in the dining room of their hotel, the very non-Argentinian-sounding Lancaster, which was nonetheless on Avenida Córdoba, a principal Buenos Aires thoroughfare. The linen-covered table for four was in a corner of the rather formal dining room, underpopulated now, as the morning waned. Sand seated himself between his wife and his onetime colleague.

Both women were in slacks and silk blouses and yet looked nothing alike, except for their general beauty. They were having eggs and bacon with coffee, just as the probable former Führer and his breakfast companion had been. Sand filled a cup from a carafe of coffee and helped himself to one of Stacey's bacon slices, which was nicely crisp—the Lancaster was not stingy with their servings.

"It does rather neatly tie up," he admitted, chewing, "the Nazi elements of this inquiry."

Both women were goggling at him with their big beautiful eyes, pool-table green ones in Stacey's case, a clear morning blue in Charlotte's.

Calmly he told them what he'd observed—that this Victor Von Koerber was a ringer for the wartime Hitler, minus only the Charlie Chaplin mustache and intervening years.

"Of course," he said, "plastic surgery already seems to be playing a major role here. The only question is whether this little group of war criminals is hiding their identities or preparing for a re-emergence. Fourth Reich anyone? More coffee?"

Stacey, perhaps suspecting this was all an elaborate put-on by her husband, said, "And I suppose his breakfast companion was Eva Braun."

"Isn't that obvious? She looked familiar to me before *he* did! Unlike *Herr Wolf*, she's aged normally, or anyway dodged the plastic surgeon's blade. Assuming she didn't die in a bunker with her husband in April 1945, Eva would be in her fifties—fifty-one, perhaps? Rather well-preserved, though."

Stacey said to Charlotte, "Perhaps he's lost his mind."

Charlotte said, "Perhaps *we* have...*Mon cher*, how can you be so casual, so calm, if such a thing *d'horrible* is true?"

"I didn't report a fact. I gave an opinion. If I were certain, I might be less casual. Less calm. I might have stormed that apartment house and starting shooting."

That rocked his wife's head back, but Charlotte only said, "This apartment house may be no ordinary one. We made no check of who else lives there, after all... and do you either of you, *mes amies*, thinking back on the comings and goings, recall more than a few Latins entering? And those who did were dressed in the uniform of the servant, *n'est-ce pas?*"

The neighborhood was wealthy, which had dictated the varied approach of how they'd watched the building— hanging around in a well-to-do area would draw attention whereas in the barrio it might not.

"They looked European to me," Stacey said, regaining her mental equilibrium, "mostly older folks. If Von Koerber really is...who you *think* he may be...he would be surrounded by supporters, and possibly members of his staff, who'd also gone underground."

Sand, pausing before selecting another strip of bacon from his wife's plate, said, "Perhaps I should order my own breakfast."

Stacey rolled her eyes and pushed her plate over to him. "Have the rest of mine."

"Thank you, darling."

Sitting forward, her food forgotten, Charlotte said, "When we spoke of a new, advanced form of plastic surgery, we speculated the replacing of a world leader on today's stage...what about one from *yesterday's* stage?"

Sand paused, mid-chew. "You mean, what if that is indeed the real Eva Braun who survived somehow...but this Hitler lookalike is Von Koerber *after* plastic surgery? Designed to make him seem the *real* Uncle Adolf? You have a devious mind, Charlotte. I've always liked that about you."

"*Merci.* And to relaunch the Reich? A credible Hitler lookalike would make such a thing possible."

Sand tossed a half-eaten bacon strip on the plate he'd confiscated from his wife. "What if that's Meier's plan?"

Stacey frowned. "What if *what's* Meier's plan?"

"He's been snatching up smuggled uranium, right?"

Both women nodded.

"Perhaps he's using Nazi scientists to construct an atomic bomb."

Stacey gestured with an open hand. "We've considered that from the start—that someone wanted enough uranium to build a bomb. Even enough to build an arsenal."

Sand raised a forefinger. "Yes, but we didn't know *why.* What if it's to start a third World War and bring about the rebirth of the Reich—with a doppelgänger Hitler as their leader? Perhaps a sane, easily handled Hitler, at that."

Stacey winced. "Invading Poland is one thing, initiating Armageddon is something else again. *No one* wants to start World War Three."

"Neither do the USA or Soviet Union, presumably," Sand said. "Each just wants to be powerful enough to threaten it."

Shaking her head, Charlotte said, "But Germany, she is split in two. They are no longer a world power, cowed as they are by the victors."

Sand smiled, though of course this was nothing to smile about, really.

"What if," he said, "Meier wants to reunite East and West Germany, with the idea of a consolidated Germany that would again rally behind his reborn Reich?"

Stacey asked, "How would he do that?"

Sand's eyes narrowed. "What did 'Hearn' say in Geneva? More or less?"

His wife's eyebrows went up and came back down. "That the power of the atom is the future. That it will liberate the citizens of the world to enjoy freedoms only the elite now possess. Raise humanity to the next level of existence. 'For the next thousand years, peace will reign.' Bunch of high-flown rhetoric."

Sand grunted a laugh. "Is it? What if Meier could use his atomic arsenal to make Germany one country again—a player in the deadliest arms race mankind has ever waged?"

Stacey's shrug lifted her shoulders high and her hands were palms up, as if daring him to fill them with something believable. "How would Meier do *that* exactly?"

"I haven't," Sand admitted, "put that together yet."

But Charlotte said, "What if an atomic bomb destroyed the wall? That very real wall that is also a symbol of what a lowly defeated thing Germany has become?"

"That's absurd," Stacey said.

But Sand was staring at the Frenchwoman. "That *is* absurd. It's a crazy, horrible thought...but it doesn't mean Meier wouldn't do it."

Stacey said, "I don't like the way you two are looking at each other. We're not attacking some Nazi apartment-house fortress, are we? I could use some sleep first."

With a dry little grin, Sand said, "Much as I would like to do just that, no. We have a theory based upon a man seen from a distance resembling a dead dictator, and little else. We need to confer with Double M. And not by phone."

* * * * * *

Within two hours they were on the Boldt Energy private plane headed back toward the United States. Their Cessna 310 had a top speed of 220 miles per hour, at about a thousand miles of range per leg of the trip, so they'd need at least six stops for fuel.

This meant two days before putting the Von Koerber conundrum on Double M's desk, which made Sand uneasy; but they had left the agents at the Buenos Aires GUILE office to maintain surveillance on the high-end apartment house, emphasizing the importance of their mission though not what made it so.

They stopped in Mexico for an overnight layover, to give Tom, their pilot, time to catch some sleep before the final leg to Vegas. They'd booked ahead rooms at the Continental Hilton and were exhausted yet wide awake when they and their bags got to their rooms at midday. Minus their dead-tired pilot, they adjourned to the hotel bar.

This time of day, the Maya Bar—a kidney-shaped island in the middle of the room, a glass wall looking out onto a garden with a corn-plant sculpture—seemed empty save for the bartender and a few businessmen at the bar. The trio took a table with under a gaily colorful Deco mural of Lake Patzcuaro, including elements of mosaic and metal relief; but their pretty waitress wore a white blouse with tuxedo pants that were more Anywhere Hilton than Mexico City.

By their third round, Sand was finishing his expected vodka martini while Stacey was staring a hole through her bourbon and Charlotte was swirling two fingers of tequila. Call it social drinking, call it self-medication, but a few drinks would help them get the sleep they hadn't managed on the plane. The few words they'd spoken thus far had not included anything regarding what they'd seen and done in Argentina.

Finally Charlotte said, "You two make a lovely couple. *Vous* êtes *si manifestement amoureux*."

Sand had enough French to realize she was commenting on how obviously he and Stacey were in love. He also knew what effect Tequila could have on Charlotte. But he wondered how much French his wife understood.

At any rate she was smiling, and lifting her glass. "And you are a *lovely* woman."

"*Merci, ma chérie,*" Charlotte said, lifting her glass to Stacey, bestowing a tiny smile. The two women clinked glasses, then threw down the rest of their drinks. Then the trio assembled whatever of their dignity and dexterity remained and made it to the elevator and up to their adjoining rooms.

Alone with his wife, Sand stripped to his boxers and drew back the covers, blessed sleep beckoning. Meanwhile, Stacey slipped into the bathroom and emerged before long in a diaphanous, spaghetti-strapped black nightgown so low-cut that her bosom overwhelmed her wardrobe.

Perhaps, he thought, *sleep was* not *the most urgent priority...*

A knock came at the adjoining door.

Stacey—possibly too tight to remember she was in a negligee with her husband in his boxers, or perhaps simply not caring—opened the door for their travel companion, who was in a baby doll so sheer the pink of her erect nipples defeated the black of the nightie. In her hands, as if an award she were about to present, was an open bottle of wine.

Charlotte went to Sand, standing alongside the bed, placed the wine bottle on the nightstand, and fell into his arms, as tipsy as he'd ever seen her. Helplessly, Sand looked at his wife like a man in choppy water who could use a life preserver. Charlotte planted tiny kisses on his neck and chest, her long dark hair tickling him, and again he turned to Stacey, wide-eyed, her mouth yawning open but not in a tired way.

Then his wife was moving toward them, presumably to break this up, but Charlotte, seeing her coming, turned to her and transferred herself to Mrs. Sand's shocked embrace.

"*Vous êtes si belle,* Stacey. So very beautiful."

Stacey looked to Sand for help, but he held his hands up in surrender.

Charlotte was slurring, "Such a long evening ahead and I am so bored. Surely there is some way to pass the time... *Je te veux tous les deux...*"

I want you both.

Stacey shook her head and her expression, and her voice, expressed nothing unkind. "Not tonight, darling."

Charlotte's sigh was elaborate. "The saddest words," she said, "in the English language."

The French woman needed help getting back into her room but Sand stayed out of it. He allowed Stacey to drunk-walk the woman into the adjacent quarters and heard, but did not see, what was likely Stacey helping their colleague into bed and tucking her in.

His wife, closing that adjacent door, said, "She's very drunk. We'll forgive her. Just this once... You don't *really* need two women, do you?"

"No," he said, and proved it to her.

Neither at breakfast in the Hilton's Café Grill Tarasco nor on the flight from Mexico City to Las Vegas had the Sands and Charlotte spoken of the inebriated near romp of the afternoon before.

Now, less than twenty-four hours later, they were in Las Vegas seated opposite Lord Marbury at the Destiny Hotel and Casino in the replica MI6 office. They had freshened up, lunched in the coffee shop, and continued to leave out yesterday's bedroom encounter as if they'd imagined it.

Sand filled Double M in concisely but completely, closing with, "Our conclusion is that Milan Meier and Kyla Fluss have undergone relatively minor but sophisticated plastic surgery. Victor Von Koerber appears to be undergoing rather more elaborate cosmetic surgery to provide a renewed Nazi movement with a facsimile of Adolf Hitler as a rallying point."

Double M said nothing, his expression unreadable. Sand would not have been surprised if his longtime boss had laughed derisively, or responded in rage at the outlandish assumptions they'd been making. Marbury might have questioned their sanity or at least their capacity for rational thinking.

Instead, their supervisor filled a pipe with tobacco and lighted it up and got it going, apparently lost in thought. Or perhaps he was waiting for a secret button he'd pushed summoning men in white coats with straitjackets at the ready to come rushing in.

Letting out fragrant smoke—Sand recognized the pleasant aroma as Mac Baren's Scottish mixture—Double M said reflectively, "There is one cosmetic surgeon who comes to mind—or at least he *was* such until his license was pulled in both Britain and the States. He was a reckless, dangerous devil who didn't believe in rules or regulations when it came to his experimental methods. His name is Aldrich Pilgrim—still widely known as the Notorious Dr. Pilgrim, despite the lack of license."

Sand shook his head. "Widely to you, sir, perhaps. The name means nothing to me."

"No reason that it should, Triple Seven. Slightly before your time, although Pilgrim's brand of politics has lingering resonance. He was a devoted follower of Oswald Mosley."

Stacey asked, "Oswald who?"

That name Sand had recognized, and said, "Mosley. British Fascist rabble-rouser going back to the '20s."

Double M let out more aromatic smoke. "That perhaps understates it. Let's just say that when Mosley married his mistress in 1936 in Berlin, Adolf Hitler was guest of honor, and the wedding took place at the home of Joseph Goebbels."

Stacey had whitened. "Wonder if Eva Braun caught

the bride's bouquet."

"She might have," Double M said, as if that had been a serious question. "She was in attendance."

Sand said, "And your Notorious Pilgrim character was a follower of Mosley's?"

"His personal physician," Double M said. "Cosmetic surgery was only one of his specialties."

Charlotte asked, "This Pilgrim, he is among the living?"

"Not certain," Double M admitted. "Pilgrim was using his techniques to aid various traitors to assume new identifies back in Kim Philby days. Shortly before he lost his license, which was perhaps ten years ago, he'd been a popular if unpublicized choice among celebrities. Operating in Mexico and South America, which obviously may be significant. With his Nazi connections, he's definitely a logical candidate here."

Sand sat forward. "What about Von Koerber?"

Double M was getting his pipe going again. "We'll step up surveillance. This potential new Nazi threat you've uncovered is not to be taken lightly—not with the likes of Josef Mengele sticking his head up out of the swamp. We'll bring every intelligence agency aligned with GUILE in on this one. In the meantime..."

"Yes?"

Double M sighed smoke. "This is a long shot, but it's somewhere for you to start, at least, and it's right here in Las Vegas. There's an entertainer who just might know the world of plastic surgery as well as just about anyone. I think talking to him would be worth your time."

"Of course," Sand said with a flip of the hand.

Their superior put his pipe in an ashtray and found a card in his Rolodex. Then he reached for his phone and punched in numbers. "...This is Malcom Marbury. Is Lee available?...Thank you...Lee, three of my people have a few questions for you..." Double M chuckled. "No, nothing to do with the IRS. My group has no affiliations there, I assure you. Just a matter you might be able to help us with...Good. Good."

Double M said goodbye and hung up, then wrote down the name and address for them.

The trio was in the elevator before a wide-eyed Sand handed Stacey the slip of paper, which Stacey—equally wide-eyed now—passed to Charlotte.

"*Liberace?*" Stacey said.

Charlotte was shrugging. "What does he do, this... Liver-achie?"

"Liber," Stacey said. "He's a piano player."

Sand said, "That's like saying Picasso paints."

The elevator chimed and they stepped into the bustling lobby at the edge of the ding-ding-dinging casino.

Stacey asked, "How in the world would Double M know Liberace?"

Sand pointed to a poster announcing the pianist's appearance in the Destiny Showroom—Extra Added Attraction: Barbra Streisand.

"Why shouldn't he?" Sand asked rhetorically. "We both know celebrities. You know John Wayne. I know Peter Lawford."

Charlotte said, "I have met the famous John Sand and his rich and famous wife."

They all smiled and shrugged. After all, Lord Malcolm Marbury knowing Lee Liberace wasn't the strangest thing that had happened to them lately.

When they arrived at 4982 Shirley Street, Sand parked a Ford sedan from the GUILE motor pool inside a wrought-iron fence separated by brick pillars, a red carpet leading from the sidewalk to the front door. With a tall palm on either side, the white stucco, black-roofed, one-story house seemed to ramble on forever.

Sand rang the bell and their wait was short, one side of a massive wood double door opening to reveal a balding butler in a black tuxedo. He might have been fifty, he might have been seventy.

"We're expected," Sand said pleasantly, and introduced himself and the two women.

The butler nodded. "This way, please, Mr. Sand, ladies." The accent wasn't exactly British, but it wasn't not exactly British, either.

They were led through an elaborately ornate, shades-of-ivory house awash with Victorian furniture, under crystal chandeliers, past two grand pianos, on their way to sliding glass doors onto a pool area in the fenced-in well-tended backyard. On a chaise lounge, wearing only gold lamé trunks, his brown hair thick and swept back, Liberace sunned himself by the pool. He looked fit.

Seeing them, Liberace sat up, removed his Ray-Bans and a vast smile blossomed, eighty-eight keys worth of even, perfect teeth minus any black notes. "Welcome, welcome. Wallace, bring our guests some lemonade, if you please."

"Right away, sir," the butler said, and dematerialized.

"You'd be Sand, John Sand," Liberace said, not rising yet gracious, extending a hand to be shaken, which his male guest did, before introducing the two females.

Now Liberace stood, taking time to wrap himself in a white terry knee-length robe before turning his high-wattage smile on them, seeming absolutely delighted to see these complete strangers.

"You are a very lucky man," their host informed Sand,

"to have two such lovely companions."

The pianist kissed the back of Stacey's hand, then Charlotte's, and escorted the little group to white metal seats at a nearby umbrella-shaded table.

"Mr. Liberace..." Sand began.

But their host cut him off. "Lee, please, call me Lee, everyone does. You're friends of Malcolm's, or is it work colleagues? I've known him for years and when he turned up at the Destiny, I thought I'd plotz."

Sand didn't know that word but the context carried it.

Stacey filled her open mouth with a few words: "Lord Marbury is 'Malcolm' to you?"

Their host's smile wasn't as broad now, though it seemed endlessly amused. "Well, it's his *name*, darling. Don't people call *you* 'Stacey?'"

"Well, yes, but I'm not royalty."

"Don't sell yourself short, dear. We're all royalty, if we strive to be. Anyway, I've read about you—the oil heiress who fills her daddy's cowboy boots. Impressive!"

"Thank you," Stacey said, but it seemed almost a question.

Turning his attention to Sand, Liberace asked, "And what brings the most famous espionage agent in the world to my humble doorstep?"

"Lord Marbury was hoping you could help us in locating a certain doctor."

"Which doctor might that be?"

"Aldrich Pilgrim."

Liberace's expression said he'd just bitten into a lemon. "Great surgeon, horrible man."

"Could you elaborate?"

The pianist lifted his face to the sun, pressed a perfectly manicured finger lightly under his chin. "He did this for me—quite amazing. There are those who say I don't look a day over...well, you tell *me*."

Charlotte said, "No more than thirty, *mon cher*."

Liberace beamed. "Thank you, darling. Such a lovely accent from such a lovely young woman."

Sand smiled inwardly. Charlotte was priming the pump.

Continuing, their host said, "No scars, no lines—perfect work, really. But the bedside manner of a snake, that man—cold-blooded and, in his case, decidedly poisonous. Not to mention the highway robbery involved."

Sand said, "He is unlicensed in the States, I understand."

"His clinic is not within our borders," Liberace said, nodding, then his eyes flared. "The entire experience was really quite bizarre."

Charlotte asked, "When was your surgery?"

"Three months ago."

"*C'est impossible!*"

"I am living proof, my dear, that it is *very* possible. He was recommended by some of the biggest names in film and on stage, who also have benefitted from the wonders this terrible man can perform. Think of it—no scarring to speak of, and faster healing than you might dream possible."

Sand asked, "Where did you last see him?"

"Not since a week after the surgery. In his clinic."

"Which is where?"

"I really don't know."

Sand frowned. "You don't know where your surgery was performed?"

"I do not. Through an intermediary, I was given a set of conditions to follow. I flew to Santiago, Chile, in a private plane, wore dark glasses and a wig and clothes that were definitely *not* my style. Pilgrim met me there, then we drove for hours, crossing the border into Argentina. He said not two civil words to me in that time! At that point I was blindfolded and conveyed to the clinic. I didn't see anything to speak of while I was prepped, and then they anaesthetized me and did the work. It wasn't until I was coming out of it that I heard one of them say that the guards were going into Bariloche as soon as the 'gringo' was out of the clinic."

Sand smiled. "You wouldn't have made a bad spy, Lee. I'm surprised Lord Marbury didn't recruit you."

The big famous smile flashed. "Coming from the most famous secret agent in the world, that means a lot."

The lemonade arrived and they sat and sipped it and chatted with their host about Las Vegas, where he'd been appearing so often, he went ahead and moved there. As the conversation wound down, Sand rose and thanked the pianist for his help.

They were back in the Ford before Charlotte asked, "How did Lord Marbury come to know this man, do you think?"

Stacey smirked. "That's probably above our security clearance."

"Some secrets," Sand said, "are best kept that way."

CHAPTER EIGHT

THE DOCTOR IS IN

In a GUILE meeting room at the Destiny—a map spread out on a round table before them—Sand, Stacey, Charlotte, and Lord Marbury stood looking down at Argentina. The country, wide at the top, tapered narrow at its southernmost point, each province given a different color by the mapmaker.

Double M straightened and puffed his pipe. "San Carlos de Bariloche is inherently problematic."

"How so?" Sand asked.

"Bariloche and the Lake Nahuel Huapi area are in a region of Argentina very much resembling Bavaria. A good number of German immigrants settled there, especially after the war, although perhaps 'good' is a poor choice of words in this instance."

Charlotte tapped that spot on the map. "The Nazis go there to hide, *n'est-ce pas?*"

Smoke fled Double M's lips as he nodded. "With the Argentinian government's blessing."

"And the people's," Sand said. "Most Argentines are of German, Spanish or Italian descent. So we will take care going in."

"But you're *not* going in," Double M said flatly. "Not initially."

"We developed this lead," Sand said, careful not to sound defensive. "Why not allow us to pursue it?"

"I *handed* you the lead," Double M said, "sending you to my friend on Shirley Street. And while your missions over the years have been notable in many ways, Triple Seven, 'taking care' has never been your hallmark."

"Rate of success," Sand said, losing the defensiveness battle, "ought to count for something."

"It does. But you and Mrs. Sand are both too well known, at this stage, to assume undercover identities, or for that matter even to maintain a low profile anywhere around Bariloche. Which, let me remind you, is all we have to go on—we do not know the location of Pilgrim's 'clinic,' other than it not being in the town itself. Nor do we know what strength of opposition awaits, and not even if the Notorious Dr. Pilgrim is at present there. This clinic of his may shift from one location to another."

"No argument," Sand admitted glumly.

Double M gestured more generally to the map. "We already have GUILE agents in country. We'll let them do the preliminary work of investigating Pilgrim and locating his clinic. Once we know what we're dealing with, you three can go in—with my blessing, and a local man...and of course sufficient armament."

"What do we do," Stacey asked, with the look of a child who stepped off a merry-go-round too soon, "in the meantime?"

With his pipe in hand, Marbury granted them benediction or perhaps absolution. "Go home, run your business, be seen in Houston. You've been away long enough. You two need to be observed living your normal lives."

Charlotte, not quite frowning, asked, "*Et pour moi?*"

"You, Agent DuBois," Double M said, "will direct the investigation from here."

Sand knew better than to argue, and anyway, Double M was right. GUILE had people in place on site to better undertake this phase of the mission; local agents would blend in where two American faux-tourists or business-people would not. But he still had something to contribute.

Pointing down at the map, he zeroed in on San Carlos de Bariloche, then followed Lake Nahuel Huapi northwest. Narrowing in on a dot at the other end of the lake from Bariloche, there it was—Inalco House.

"That's Von Koerber's estate," he said.

"You know this how?" Double M asked.

"That's according to Ambassador Northam. How far is Inalco from Bariloche?"

"Less than one hundred kilometers."

Turning to Charlotte, Sand said, "Start the search on that side of Bariloche. It's a good bet Pilgrim's clinic is somewhere between Von Koerber's estate and the town."

Charlotte nodded. "*C'est logique.*"

With his palms open, his arms outstretched, Marbury said to the Sands, "Your insights are appreciated, Triple Seven... Now, go home, you two. Take a night in Sin City if you must, but then get rest, live your lives. Take a bore-dom break. As soon as we have something, either Miss DuBois or I will contact you."

* * * * * *

Mr. and Mrs. Sand didn't bother to spend the night in Vegas; they'd had more than enough of "Lost Wages," as the lounge comics called it. Boldt Company pilot Tom had them back in the air and heading home before dark. When they landed in Houston, their chauffeur, butler and bodyguard approached them on the tarmac, and they were all one man: former *federale* Ernesto Cuchillo.

Barely taller than Stacey, Cuchillo—his skin the color and consistency of an old saddle, his black hair long and tied in a ponytail—gave them a big grin, which in his case meant the thin lips of his pockmarked face curling almost imperceptibly upward at the corners.

"*Bienvenida de vuelta*," Cuchillo said.

"Good to be back," Sand said, and shook the man's hand, after which Stacey gave him a hug, Cuchillo's duties having once included being the Boldt girl's "nanny."

Cuchillo loaded the couple's luggage into the trunk of their big black Cadillac, and before long they were cruising up the long private drive to the home Stacey's mother had christened *Plata Luna*—Silver Moon. The ranch was the first place Sand had lived since his childhood that really felt as such—even the pleasures of his swank London apartment paled. Of course, it didn't hurt that his wife was a beautiful, rich woman.

"What are you smiling about?" Stacey asked.

"Just thinking what a simple soul I've become," he said.

After the travel of these past days, they went to bed without even unpacking, sleeping in late. The day that awaited them immediately drew the couple into their routine as energy company executives. Stacey went to meetings, Sand made trips to vendors and customers, who were excited to be in the presence of a sort of celebrity. Double M called once a week at a set time, but had no news to share, or at least he didn't share any. Sand called Charlotte every few days.

"Anything?" he would ask.

"*Mon cher*," she would say, "the communication from the woods and mountains...*est insuffisante et contradictoire.* What is learned from the little towns is not much better. "

The local agents Double M had found preferable to sending Sand and company in had not found the clinic yet. That rankled.

As the days passed, Sand and Stacey worked and occasionally went out to dinner, but mostly stayed home. Anxiety was tearing away at him, one strip of skin at a time. He sensed Stacey felt similarly, but she hid it well. He hoped the same was true for himself.

Having dinner on the patio one night, two days until Halloween, two months since they'd left GUILE HQ, Vegas and Charlotte behind, with the orange ball of sun dying its screamingly beautiful death at the horizon, Sand pushed away a plate of food bearing more of his blood-red filet than he'd eaten.

Cuchillo exchanged the plate for a vodka martini and Sand nodded his thanks as the major domo disappeared.

"No appetite?" Stacey asked.

"None to speak of," he said.

"But you *do* have."

"Have what?"

"An appetite." She was trying to keep it light and failing. "To be anywhere else but here."

"Not true." He put his hand on hers. "There's nowhere I'd rather be, it's just..."

"What?"

His grimace came and went. But that it had come at all lingered. "I don't like being pulled off the front line. Not when something this big is in the offing."

She sipped her glass of Rosé. "Nazis, atomic bombs, assassins, old lovers, you mean?"

"Living our normal life right now just doesn't feel right. Double M, damnit, is wasting us."

She arched an eyebrow. "You mean, he's wasting *you*, don't you?"

"No. Both of us." He sighed. "The people out there living a normal life...and I admit *our* normal is special, even rarefied...are simply not aware the world is on fire."

"Isn't it always, John?"

"It is. It's just...at this moment I can feel the flames on my face..."

She put some baby talk into her reply. "And you want to put on your little fireman's hat, don't you?"

He might have been offended, but only laughed. "I guess I'm not the only fireman in the world, am I?"

Another sip. "No. There are other people like you, perhaps not as...'rarefied'...but they do the job. And there's a capable few in your league—Double M, for instance, and your friend Charlotte."

"*Our* friend."

"Our friend." Her turn to sigh; she leaned near him. Were there tears in her eyes? "And you did your best, John. You really did mean to retire from the spy life and lean comfortably back and become a man of leisure..."

"A kept man," he said with a smile.

"*Well*-kept at that. But your old life kept intruding on your new one, and I had to either let go of you or join you. And that's what I've done. If you're the 'Guy from GUILE,' I'm the 'Gal from Guile,' graduating with honors. Except for one damn manikin."

"You're remarkable, Stacey Sand." He raised his martini glass to her. "You really are."

"I know it. Now, if *I* can just adjust to the frantic, dangerous things the fire alarms announce, and go along for the wild ride, *you* can surely adjust to the down times between, here at the ranch. In other words, if I can be a part-time secret agent, you can be a part-time oil company executive. Okay, cowboy?"

She leaned near enough to kiss him lightly. He slipped an arm around her and damn near pulled her off her chair to give her the kind of kiss she deserved.

Cuchillo cleared his throat.

Sand drew away from his beautiful wife, a few inches anyway, and looked up at the big small man.

"My apologies, but Miss DuBois is on the phone."

As Sand followed Cuchillo toward the house, Stacey's voice chased him. "Tell that woman she has lousy timing!"

Cuchillo had left the receiver in the kitchen on the counter. Sand picked it up. "Yes?"

Charlotte said, "We *found* it, John."

Excitement spiked in him. "The clinic?"

"*Oui*, but Pilgrim, he is not there."

And just as quickly deflated. "Hell you say."

"No, but soon he should be. Word is he will return in one week. *C'est une bonne* intel! You remember our man—Jaime? He gather this himself. It will take us most of that time to get there. Lord Marbury requests you and Stacey meet with us at the Destiny mid-morning. Can you manage that?"

Stacey was poised in the kitchen doorway, looking at him expectantly.

He nodded. "We'll be there."

After he'd hung up, she said, "Fire alarm?"

Another nod. "Call Tom. Fly out to Vegas early tomorrow. I'll start packing. Meet me in the bedroom."

Her smile was small but hugely wicked. "Try to stop me."

* * * * * *

The next day, Double M and Charlotte were waiting for the couple in the same GUILE meeting room, the map of Argentina again spread out on the table. Double M wore a dark gray pristine pinstripe, Charlotte a light blue blouse and navy slacks coincidentally echoing Stacey's similar attire in pink and red. Anticipating travel, Sand was in a Brooks Brothers sports jacket, Ban-Lon shirt and Sansabelt slacks in tones of brown.

Using a wooden pointer, Double M said, "There's a good reason why it took so long to find this damned clinic. We assumed it was near Bariloche when it's halfway between Von Koerber's estate and there. Middle of nowhere, actually. John, if you hadn't learned of the estate and advised Charlotte where to look, we might still be beating the bullrushes for the blasted thing."

"We go today?" Sand asked.

Marbury shook his head. "No. You need detailed briefing in preparation for what lies ahead."

Twenty-some hours passed before the three agents took off for Buenos Aires, and another two days passed before they landed in the capital of Argentina, where local GUILE agent, Jaime, met them on the tarmac. He wore the same navy-blue suit he'd been wearing when Sand saw first him in the bullet-proof glass box where the young man had been eating a *Bauru* sandwich.

Sand shook hands with the agent, who before had always been seated at the watchdog desk. Turned out Jaime was almost as tall as Sand, if rail thin. His mahogany skin had a glow in the bright sunlight, his black hair noticeably longer with a wispy mustache and beard added, the rewards of time in the timberland.

As they headed into the airport, Sand said, "I understand you collected all that intel for us about the clinic."

The young man grinned shyly. "Yes, sir."

"And here I assumed you weren't ripe enough for field work."

"People underestimate me because of my age, Mr. Sand. It can be an advantage."

"Well, use it as long as you can. Ready to take us in country?"

"We should change first. It is an arduous trip up into the mountains."

He drove them to the shabby brick facade of the Buenos Aires GUILE office and, when they reemerged, all four were wearing fatigues and combat boots. The first leg of their journey would be via a Jeep waiting in the modest parking lot. Jaime drove, Sand took the passenger seat, and the two women snugged in back. The trip was almost sixteen hundred kilometers, good road starting out, ever less so as they went.

As they started out, Jaime filled them in on the layout of the grounds of the clinic.

"There is something," the young agent added, obviously uneasy, "we did not anticipate."

"What's that?" Sand asked.

Dark eyebrows rose and lowered. "There was talk of 'shadow people' in the hills. The doctor...he did things to these people."

Sand frowned. "What sort of things?"

"No one would say, nothing *definido*...but they speak in hushed tones as you would of the very sick...or the dead." He shivered in the heat. *"Fue muy aterrador."*

"Frightening how?" Sand asked.

"No one would say what happens in that terrible place... but the fear on their faces spoke much." He glanced at the

British agent. "That is frightening, of itself, is it not?"

"It is indeed."

Eleven-hundred kilometers from Buenos Aires was Neuquen, the province capital where they took rooms for the night in a modern hotel, with none of the Mexico City nonsense ensuing. Early the next morning they were on their way again; after skirting Bariloche, they got onto a mostly paved two-lane road that led toward Inalco House at the far end of Lake Nahuel Huapi.

A cool afternoon settled over the forest-covered mountains bordering the lake. Bariloche was forty-some kilometers in the rearview mirror when Jaime pulled off the road and onto an unpaved dirt path into the woods.

A kilometer later, dust kicking up behind them, the driver veered off between two trees, the Jeep bouncing over exposed roots as they went cross-country. When they were well out of sight of the dirt road, Jaime finally stopped the Jeep.

"From here," he said, "we walk."

They climbed out and gathered their gear. All four had M1 Garand rifles as well as sidearms; in addition to his Walther, Sand had his Beretta in an ankle holster and a switchblade in a pocket. The two men grabbed backpacks with some food, canteens, binoculars, and a few hand grenades, just in case things got interesting.

Sand asked, "How far?"

Jaime pointed north. "Three kilometers to the clinic, maybe two and a half till we come onto guards."

One eyebrow up, Stacey said, "Run that by us one more time, would you?"

Jaime's nod was respectful. "There are six armed guards when Pilgrim is not on site. One on each corner of the building, two rovers who maintain about half a click distance from the building. They communicate by walkie-talkie."

Charlotte said, "But the doctor will be there now, *oui*?"

Jaime nodded. "Should be, unless things have changed since my return and our trip here. Pilgrim's presence adds a personal security crew of three. All are former *Waffen* SS—well-trained marksmen and fighters."

Stacey said, "So we're facing nine trained killers."

"The regular guards are less well-trained. They have basic skills, but it is Dr. Pilgrim's security team who are the trained killers."

Beneath a certain bravado, Jaime seemed tense.

Sand asked, "Is this your first dangerous mission, son?"

The young man shook his head. "No. Not at all. But for this one, I admit an...uneasiness."

Stacey said, "Because of the shadow people?"

"*Sí*," Jaime said. "*They* are afraid, so *I* feel...*un poco nervioso*."

Charlotte said, "A little fear is not a bad thing."

"We take out the two roving guards," Sand said, not caring much for such talk. "Jaime, as the only native Spanish speaker, you'll collect both walkies. Should they check on your status, keep your responses clipped—the more you say, the more chance they'll tip to a voice that seems wrong."

Jaime nodded.

"All right," Sand said. "Let's make this Jeep disappear."

They used branches and leaves to camouflage the vehicle, then they moved off through the trees and brush. Familiar with the terrain, Jaime led the way, Sand next, Stacey, then Charlotte, the latter tasked with making sure no one came up behind them...not even the shadow people. They moved slowly, all but silently, and twenty minutes later were a kilometer away from the clinic, half a click from where they'd likely be encountering guards.

Then Jaime froze, holding up a hand.

He pointed—maybe twenty meters ahead, a guard had his back to them. They lowered themselves to the ground, flat on their stomachs. Sand gave Jaime a look that said, *I'll handle this,* got out the switchblade, opened it here where its click could be swallowed by general wildwood noise. While the other three waited, Sand crawled on his belly till he was within a meter of the guard. He was weighing whether to throw the knife or get close enough to stab or slash when the guard sauntered off through the trees.

Sand lifted to a knee. He slowly scanned the woods and saw nothing. He waved the others forward to his position.

"Don't know who was luckier," Stacey said to Sand. "You or that guard."

To Jaime, Sand said, "That was half a kilometer too soon."

The young man shrugged. "Before, the rovers were always another half kilometer closer to the clinic."

Up ahead two more men were talking. Again, the quartet ate dirt. Two more sentries strolled so near that Sand could smell them, then the pair veered off—headed in the opposite direction their compatriot had gone.

Sand whispered, "They've more than doubled the guard."

Charlotte was shaking her head. "Do we back off now, until we know more?"

Before that question could be answered, a sound came from the dirt road they'd come in on. Still on the ground, Sand shimmied out of his backpack, got the binoculars out, and tried to focus the glasses through the trees at the car on that road.

A clear view was difficult, as the vehicle moved fast—a gray Mercedes convertible. Two men in front and two more in back—and in the passenger seat was Milan Meier. Passing the binoculars to Stacey, he whispered, "See anyone you know?"

She held the binoculars up, adjusted them slightly, then whispered, "Well. Jackpot."

"What is it?" Charlotte asked.

"Hearn," Stacey said. "That is...Meier. He's in that Mercedes."

Sand said, "Which is why there's more security—the top man is here."

Charlotte asked, "As the patient? Or the big boss man?"

"Not our concern," Sand said, and sent his eyes around to each of them. "We have a choice—back off because of this increased security, or take advantage of getting Meier and Pilgrim at the same time."

Jaime asked, "It's your decision, Señor Sand. You are the agent in charge."

But Sand was looking at two women, both younger than himself, each extraordinarily dear to him, knowing he'd be putting them at even more risk than this mission had required prior to this change of circumstance.

"We can return to Buenos Aires and assemble a larger team," he said. "Mercenaries, if not enough agents are available."

"We would," Charlotte said, "lose days, *mon ami.*"

Stacey said, "And this visit from Meier may be brief—if he's not here as a patient, just checking up on things, he could easily be gone tomorrow. Even later today."

Sand studied her. "You're saying...?"

"We need to do this," his wife said.

Nodding, Charlotte said, "*Oui,* we must take the

chance, I agree."

Jaime said, "I am not anxious to make this trek another time. Let's do what we came for."

Soon they were crawling forward through high grass, moving slow, staying low. They managed to avoid the rovers, and got close enough to see the clinic through the trees—a one-story concrete building. Half a dozen armed men were hanging around outside. Adding in the roving sentries, and an unknown number inside, the tiny assault team was facing perhaps two dozen opponents.

The gray Mercedes convertible was parked on a gravel apron, as was a black Mercedes sedan with two pickup trucks parked nearby. The bunker-like building had a flat roof, a window on either side of the front door, another on the side nearest them, frosted glass on the bottom, clear on the top. Apparently Dr. Pilgrim wanted light but not prying eyes.

The plethora of security loitering outside included neither Pilgrim nor Meier, meaning the two main men were inside unless they'd taken an unlikely forest stroll.

A plan in mind now, Sand directed a retreat far enough away from the roaming sentries to risk whispered instructions.

"Stacey," Sand whispered, "you and Jaime stay put. Charlotte and I will disable the roaming sentries and return. Then the four of us will get close to the clinic again. I'll lob a grenade into Meier's car. When it goes off, it will get the sentries' attention and send them hither and yon...and will be your signal to start taking them out. Any one of them that isn't Pilgrim or Meier, shoot them and I prefer head shots. They may be wearing body armor and, anyway, they won't cry out with their brains shut off. Any questions?"

This little speech paled the two women for a moment, even Charlotte; but then they all shook their heads.

"Good," Sand said. "Charlotte, shall we?"

"With pleasure, *mon ami*. Let us even up the odds."

Leaving their rifles behind, Sand and the French agent took off in opposite directions. He had his switchblade out, skulking through the forest, staying low. The first sentry he spotted was alone. Sand worked his way around until he was behind the man, then rushed him, hand over mouth, slitting the sentry's throat, blood spraying away from both victim and his killer, the result dripping scarlet from leaves and branches. The man went limp, dead before he dropped to the ground in an undignified pile.

The next two were together, a trickier proposition. His Walther was noise-suppressed, but despite films and television, there was no such thing as true silencing and the cough the gun would make might carry and be recognized for what it was. The better part of discretion was to pursue other, more basic means.

From the forest floor he selected a rock that filled his hand nicely, and rushed the two guards from behind. Stunned to hear someone running at them, they turned, the first guard spinning; Sand smashed the man's face in with the rock, the bones of his nose driven into his brain, and he too was dead before falling to the grass. Sand, letting the mini boulder drop, tackled the second sentry at the waist, lifting him up and then driving him to the ground onto his back. As the man landed with a *whomp*, all the air left his body, while Sand rolled to one side so that when he slit the man's throat, the spray would not drench the switchblade's owner in glistening red. Instead the geyser rose and fell to make a grotesquely festive mess of the dead man. Sand had avoided most but not all of the spatter.

He continued his efforts.

Two more guards—each on solo patrol—fell to his switchblade, and then he was moving to the far side of the clinic where he met up with Charlotte. She was even more speckled with blood than he was. He wondered if his eyes were as wide and insane as hers at this moment.

"It is done," she said. *"Six hommes sont allés chez leur créateur."*

"I sent only five to meet St. Peter."

"Did you miss one?"

He looked back. "I don't think so. I didn't see another. It didn't seem that well-organized—more scattershot."

Charlotte had confiscated a walkie-talkie.

"Any chatter?" he asked.

"What is the expression? Not a peep."

"*Bon,*" he said. "Let's get moving. There's much still to be done."

CHAPTER NINE

HOUSE CALL
___

When Sand and Charlotte rejoined Stacey and Jaime kneeling in the underbrush, Mrs. Sand's eyes widened as she took in the red splatter decorating the fatigues of the arrivals.

"None of this is ours," Sand assured his wife, gesturing to the blood spots, as he and the French agent took a knee.

"You've been busy," Stacey observed.

"We have." He brought his hands together in a silent clap. "So. The guards have been dealt with. But stay sharp—might be a stray here or there. Everybody with the program?"

Nods from the rest.

"Shall we proceed?"

Another round of nods.

Rifles in hand, they moved in. No further stray roving sentries presented themselves. Staying at the edge of the woods, Sand circled the front of the clinic while the other three spread out within the barest confines of cover to give themselves a wider field of fire. Cutting across the gravel apron to get closer to the cars would be reckless. A better option was to creep farther along the fringe of the woods, take aim at the convertible, pull the pin and throw the grenade in a high arc so that it might land in the backseat.

Which he did, and it did.

As the metallic pineapple traveled through the air, he heard a guard say, "*Que es esto?*"

Another had just enough time to yell, "*Bomba!*"

The grenade plopped into the car's backseat and half a second later detonated. Shrapnel flew as the car's tail lifted off the ground and dropped with a resounding *thud*, half of the vehicle a sudden smoking snarl of steel. The guards elevated momentarily and sat back down hard on their asses; several were dead already, but one sat on the ground, legs splayed wide, a slice of smoking metal in his chest, the pistil of a crimson blooming flower. He looked dumbfounded, then his chin sagged and he joined the others in death.

Guards came around the bunker with their rifles ready, but the four attackers at the forest's edge were readier, unleashing an immediate M1 barrage. More guards fell and a few were so spooked they dropped their weapons and ran for their lives into the trees and away from the line of fire. The *Waffen* SS killers of Pilgrim's security team poured out returning fire, one with a machine gun, another a two-gun kid with a pair of blazing revolvers; but Sand took both out, coolly, one head shot at a time.

Meier, in his tinted glasses and a vaguely militaristic gray suit, stuck his head out, a pistol poised, and Sand blasted a hole inches from the man's face, splintering wood in the half-open door. The surviving SS guard, still within the building, yanked Meier back inside even as Sand and his team inched forward.

A few guards were still returning fire, but Stacey,

Jaime, and Charlotte were picking them off one at a time like carnival targets.

Then Charlotte shouted, "Meier is fleeing out the back!"

She took off after him and his SS bodyguard, with Jaime on her heels. Sand and Stacey made their way to either side of the clinic's bullet-gouged front door.

In Spanish, Sand yelled, "You're surrounded, surrender! Drop your weapons and come out, hands up!"

Two guards obeyed, fingers interlaced behind their heads. While Stacey covered them, Sand entered the bunker...

...*only to be blown back out through the door!*

On the ground, ears ringing, body one continuous ache, Sand blinked and blinked, trying to reorient. When his vision finally cleared, he looked up to see Stacey's lovely features twisted with concern, her mouth working but he couldn't hear any words, until slowly the sounds found their way through the fog.

"John, are you all right? Are you hurt?"

Getting into a sitting position with her help, he asked, "The two guards?"

"They ran when the bomb went off."

"Bomb?"

She nodded toward the clinic, where black smoke streamed out of the open door and broken windows. Sand took stock of himself—he seemed to have been hit by nothing but the shock wave of it.

Rising to wobbly feet, with Stacey lending support, Sand edged forward and they went inside into a sort of waiting room area. Broken chairs and a shattered lamp had been scattered around by the blast. Just ahead was the doorless mouth to a central hallway. Close together, her right arm around his waist, they moved down the hall, Sand not so stunned that he didn't fill his right hand with his Walther.

A door at left had been blown off, revealing an empty chamber with stands and trays and an operating table toppled. Across the way another door had been blown away, its fragments on the hallway floor; within was an office, and the doctor was in, all right—but so was a bullet in his temple by way of apparent self-medication. Probably taking the trip post-mortem, he lay knocked against the wall opposite his row of metal file cabinets, which were barely recognizable as such, just tall stalks of gnarled, scorched steel, like some awful modernistic sculpture.

"That's where the bomb went off," Sand said. "A safeguard in case they were overwhelmed."

Pieces of paper floated on the smoky air, charred confetti celebrating disaster; little fires burned in the file-cabinet husks. The office reeked of cordite.

"You're no bloody help," Sand said, looking down at Pilgrim's corpse, "are you?" To his wife, he said, "Maybe there are a few surviving documents to give us something for the effort."

Stacey shook her head, sympathetically. "John, it's no use. Everything's been blown to hell. There's nothing to save."

He pounded the nearby wooden desk once, unleashed an expletive he rarely used in front of his wife, then walked around and righted the nearly undamaged chair Pilgrim had apparently been blown out of; then he dropped into it. Anything on top of the desk had been carried away, and shrapnel had splintered the side nearest the filing cabinets, even breaking off one of the legs, leaving a sinking ship listing to that corner.

On autopilot now, enraged by how little they'd accomplished, and still shaken by the blast, Sand reached for the center desk drawer, already partly open—likely because Pilgrim had helped himself to a gun to achieve his final goal.

"*John!*" Stacey blurted. "Is that safe?"

He paused for a moment, collected his thoughts, then said, "The good doctor had the file cabinets rigged to go up. But he wouldn't risk having his desk blow up on him."

"Are you sure?"

"Quite. Uh...step outside and look for any sign of Charlotte and Jaime, would you? Rifle at the ready."

She clearly knew he meant to protect her, should he be wrong, but—after a moment—she complied.

The center drawer offered pens, paperclips, a few unimportant letters, a small screwdriver, nothing of real interest. The top drawer on the left side, however, rewarded his search with a photograph album filled with hideous pictures of human experiments gone wrong.

Clearly, Pilgrim had not limited himself to practicing plastic surgery, but was also trying to genetically improve humans with animal tissue. Thus far the results appeared disastrous, at best. H.G. Wells had not intended *The Island of Dr. Moreau* to be utilized as a how-to book.

Sickened, Sand set the album aside.

In the second drawer, he found a bottle of cheap whiskey and two shot glasses. He had a sudden vision of Dr. Pilgrim sitting at the desk alone, thumbing through the picture album as he nursed a whiskey. Did the monster ponder where his experiments might have gone awry, or was the man so far gone he thought he was doing the world some benefit?

A few photos showed the doctor, his staff, and a visiting physician—Dr. Josef Mengele—at work on projects that were as twisted as the explosion-racked file cabinets.

The third drawer, the bottom one, was empty. He checked for a false bottom—no. He pulled the drawer out and looked it over, fore and aft and underneath. Not a bloody thing. Shit! He grabbed the drawer in both hands, got to his feet, and was about to heave it at the office wall when Stacey appeared in the doorway and commented, "Whatcha up to there, big boy?...And something's off about the bottom of that drawer."

Sand looked at her, wondering if she'd been nearby in the hall all along, then flipped the drawer over for a closer look. Indeed, the bottom of the drawer appeared to have been added on, the wood dissimilar, and attached with screws. Using the screwdriver from the middle desk drawer, he removed the false bottom and a narrow wooden box slipped out, a perfect size for file folders.

He glanced at Stacey, still in the doorway, her eyes wide as he laid this secondary, hidden-away box on the desk, and slid the lid off in its grooves, revealing space for three file folders. The top one was stamped **Fluss/Rivers**, the second **Meier/Hearn**, the third **HW/Von Koerber**.

He sat at the cockeyed desk again and thumbed through Kyla's file, finding before-and-after photos, notes on the cosmetic surgeries, more notes on what Pilgrim learned that might help him in future procedures. Similar information awaited in Meier's file. The third file stopped Sand cold.

"What is it?" Stacey asked.

"Von Koerber's name is in second position."

"Is that significant?"

"The other files list patient first and assumed identity second."

"Which means what, do you think?"

"It may mean someone with the initials 'HW' is the patient, and Von Koerber is the identity to be assumed."

She just shrugged as he replaced the folders in the box and slid the lid back into the grooves.

He asked, "No sign of Charlotte and Jaime?"

"Not since they took off after Meier. I hope they haven't run into anything they can't handle."

"They'll do fine." Sand tucked the wooden box under his arm and went to Stacy, in the hall just outside the office now.

"We'll check out the rest of this torture chamber," he told her, "while we wait for them." Trying to find the others prematurely only risked getting further separated.

The remaining rooms had taken none of the explosion's impact, doors intact and unlocked, revealing a laboratory out of an old horror picture, a second operating room, a washroom, but no second office and no storage of records or other documents. Only one door remained, marked *Suministros*—Supplies.

Locked.

"Stand back," Sand said, his Walther ready to shoot the lock, when Stacy clutched his shoulder—the door was cracking open!

"Come out slowly," Sand advised sternly, putting himself between Stacey and the door, "and show me empty hands."

The door froze in its barely open position, but Sand heard whispering in Spanish, not quite making out the words.

He repeated his warning, this time in Spanish—louder.

Something clunked onto the floor, then a bare foot pushed a nine-millimeter pistol out into the room, but not just any bare foot—an unusually hairy one with dark, oddly curving toenails.

Stacey, behind her husband, gripped his left arm.

A man, or perhaps more accurately what had once been

a man, stepped out. Nearly as tall as Sand, he wore only thin gray cotton pants, otherwise naked but for a light if distinct layer of hair—almost...fur. His nose protruded enough to suggest a feline snout, and the whiskers of his mustache were stiff and gray. Stacey's hand squeezed hard.

The cat-like man had his hands still in the air, fingertips bearing razor sharp claws. Behind him a woman clung to his arm much as Stacey did Sand's, a sadly dignified figure with a simian cast to her features, her large breasts bulging a peasant top, a green skirt that dragging on the floor.

In Spanish, the feline man said, "My name is Juan Pablo Martinez. This is Lucia, my wife. I surrender. I admit killing Dr. Pilgrim. I knew where he kept his gun. And in the *confusión*, I took advantage. I shot the *demonio* in his head for what he did to us."

Not a suicide, then, driven by the GUILE team's attack. Rather, a murder, or...an execution?

"You acted fast," Sand said.

Embarrassed, Juan Pablo said, "The scent of your party preceded you, *señor*—perfume of the women, sweat of the men, and then came the gunfire. I saw a chance for justice and I took it."

Sand holstered his Walther. Still in Spanish, he said, "We mean you no harm, but the man you killed took with him the answers to many questions."

Juan Pablo's shrug was apologetic, and rather shy. "I am sorry for that, but not sorry for what I did."

"I understand. Perhaps you can help. The man in the office with Pilgrim today—did you overhear any conversation between them?"

"*Sí.* I was sweeping up. They pay no attention to me, I am in and out. They were talking about something I don't understand—an English word? Wreck?"

Reich?

"I do not know what that means," Juan Pablo continued. "Since my treatments, many things are unclear for me. Lucia can no longer speak at all. They have made monsters of us, señor, and I do as monsters do—I kill him."

"Anything you can remember them saying might help, Juan."

He rubbed his furry brow. "Something about a shipment. A second shipment of...of material. Nearly 'ready to set sail.' Nothing else. I am sorry."

Sand put a hand on the man's shoulder. "You and your wife should come with us. We'll get you help. The doctor's people may come here and see what's happened and blame you for it."

Juan Pablo's smile was entirely human. "We cannot go with you, *amigo.* What would become of us? Where would we go, what would we do? They have made monsters of us, and monsters are all we can be. And we are not alone. Others of us, friends, families...they were experiments, too. And not as successful as Lucia and I."

The terrible pictures in the album flashed through Sand's mind.

"The shadow people," Stacey whispered.

Juan Pablo nodded. "*Sí, la gente sombría.* They live in the hills. Who would care for them if not us?"

Sand looked at Stacey, her eyes glistening with sympathy. He went back to gather the photo album and the wooden box and rejoined his wife and the couple in the hallway, Lucia at her husband's side now, his arm around her.

Sand shook the man's hand, a firm grip, the clawed fingertips brushing only gently as they shook. "You should return to your friends," he told them. "While we wait for ours."

Juan Pablo's nostrils flared. "The other woman...she

is close. Be careful, *amigos*. She carries death with her."

Stacey took Lucia's hand in hers and said to the man, in Spanish: "*Matar a un demonio no es pecado.*"

To kill a demon is no sin.

As Juan's wife foraged in the rubble, Sand and Stacey stepped outside, Juan Pablo following, gathering firearms and ammunition—possibly to protect his people "in the hills," or perhaps to watch and wait for the dead doctor's allies and take more revenge. Sand was fine with either choice. But with black smoke curling in the air, easily seen from Inalco House, someone, sooner rather than later, would come.

Sand was about to suggest to Stacey that they begin a search for their comrades when they spotted Charlotte: off to one side, near the doctor's mostly undamaged car, she sat on the gravel of the apron, weeping. Jaime was sprawled on his stomach next to her. He did not appear to be breathing.

Sand confirmed it: Jaime was dead, all right.

Crouching next to Charlotte, Sand said, "Tell me."

Her breath was coming hard, half-exhaustion, half-emotion. "We were chasing them, Meier and his bodyguard. We lost them in the woods, then we caught sight of him again, Meier, running up ahead. We took pursuit. A shot came from behind us and Jaime...Jaime caught a round."

"The bodyguard," Sand said, clenching a fist. "Meier set up an ambush."

"And it worked," Charlotte said. "I should have seen it coming! *Je suis tellement stupide!* I fire back in that direction, but then they are both gone. Jaime, he was still breathing. I walked him back till he pass out, then carry him on my shoulders."

Stacey wasn't saying anything.

"What of Pilgrim?" Charlotte asked.

"Dead before we got to him."

"So," she said dejectedly, "this was all for nothing?"

"Not completely. These tell a story." He indicated the wooden box and the photo album under his left arm.

"Who is that creature?" Charlotte asked, frowning as if her eyes were lying, watching Juan Pablo gather weapons.

"One of the mad doctor's more 'successful' experiments. That and the rest of it can wait. We need to get Jaime into the back of the late doctor's car and ourselves out of here before the Nazi glee club shows up to sing 'Smoke Gets in Your Eyes.'"

The keys were in the Mercedes sedan. Sand unlocked the boot and gently as possible they loaded Jaime's body within. Sand got behind the wheel, Stacey took the passenger seat, with the photo album and wooden box between them; Charlotte crawled in back, no longer weeping but dazed, perhaps in shock.

When they made it to where Jaime had pulled the Jeep off the road, Charlotte came alive and got out to scurry and retrieve the vehicle. Then the Mercedes was moving again as the French agent disappeared into the woods to fetch the Jeep.

After a while, Stacey said, "Do you believe her?"

Sand nodded. "Why would I not?"

"Because Jaime got shot in the back."

"In an ambush."

"So she says."

They were skirting Bariloche now, headed back to Buenos Aires, Sand watching for Charlotte in the rearview mirror. He was driving just below the speed limit, only partially because he was looking for their fellow agent to catch up. Wouldn't do to get picked up for speeding with a body in the boot.

"Over the last twenty years," Sand said, "I've had my life in Charlotte's hands any number of times. And I still seem to be breathing."

"That's more than can be said for Jaime," Stacey said. "She was the sole survivor of the massacre at GUILE headquarters last year, and now she's alone with Jaime and he's shot in the back. So I have to wonder."

"I trust her."

"Your prerogative."

Charlotte finally caught up with them on the far side of Neuquen. They stopped briefly for gas and such, and, as Charlotte seemed herself again, their little caravan journeyed on.

In Buenos Aires they went directly to GUILE headquarters where they checked the Jeep in while agents took possession of both Pilgrim's vehicle and Jaime's remains. The Sands and Charlotte changed out of their fatigues into street clothes and caught a cab to a hotel. After cleaning up, they gathered in the Sands' room. Dead sober, this time.

"This is *répugnante*," Charlotte said as she slammed shut the grotesque photo album. "What kind of monster was this damn *docteur*?"

She was in a white-towel turban and white terry robe, seated at a round table in the corner, Sand at a writing desk, Stacey on the bed, her back against the headboard, similarly turbaned. Husband and wife wore white terry hotel robes, too.

"The kind of *docteur*," Sand said, "who sends you to Dr. Mengele for a second opinion. What do that quack's files tell you?"

Charlotte shrugged. "They confirm minor plastic surgery on Meier and Fluss. So little for so much trouble."

Sand shrugged. "Well, we stopped Pilgrim's progress,

at least, in the Dr. Frankenstein department. He won't be torturing and experimenting on the natives for fun and profit anymore. But that's secondary."

Stacey blinked at him. "It is?"

Sand nodded. "We've been operating under the assumption that Meier was using Pilgrim to create a facsimile Adolph Hitler by way of plastic surgery on Von Koerber, preparing him to take on the role."

Both women were sitting forward now, eyes on him as if he were about to reveal the secret of life.

"What this file indicates," Sand said, hefting the folder, "is that what they were doing was taking an *older* man and performing advance cosmetic surgery to make him look *younger.*"

Charlotte said, "Hardly unusual."

"You saw Von Koerber with his wife," Sand reminded the French agent. "You said he moved like an older man, yet when *I* saw him? He appeared to be around the same age as she did."

Stacey said, "The initials on the file were Von Koerber's and 'H.W.'"

"I believe that's one person. Von Koerber is having plastic surgery to appear younger, the same age as his fifty-year-old wife—Eva Braun."

Stacey said nothing, but her frown was eloquent.

Shaking her head, Charlotte asked, "What am I not seeing?"

"H.W.—Herr Wolf as he was sometimes called—was twenty years older than Fräulein Braun when they married. Now they appear to be the same age. I am convinced the man Dr. Pilgrim has been doing plastic surgery on, before we so rudely interrupted, is the very-real-still-breathing-didn't-kill-himself-in-the-bunker...Adolf Hitler."

CHAPTER TEN

FUTURE SHOCK

————

The trio in terry cloth now shared the round table in the Sands' hotel room, the files liberated from Pilgrim's desk spread out, their contents like bizarre cards in a high-stakes game whose rules remained uncertain.

Charlotte's voice lacked her usual confidence and had an almost little girl quality. "Could it be possible? That this foul monster and his bride from Hell did not kill themselves?"

Sand said, "You've studied this as much as I have, Charlotte—you know damn well only three people gave any kind of witness statements about the deaths of Hitler and Braun...the *Fuhrer*'s adjutant Otto Günsche, his valet Heinz Linge, and his driver Eric Kempka, head of the motor pool providing the petrol that burned the corpses. All three had identical stories and no one else ever questioned them. The Russians collected the burned bodies from the grave, but have never officially confirmed the bodies were Adolf and his Eva."

Stacey said, "I've heard my whole life that Hitler and his wife took cyanide in that bunker."

"Doesn't make it true, darling. In fact, at the Potsdam Conference when Marshal Georgy Zhukov was asked how Hitler died, Zhukov said that der Führer was alive somewhere in either Spain or Argentina. Given that a German U-boat showed up in Mar del Plata three months after the German surrender, there's enough circumstantial evidence to say we can't dismiss out of hand that we really are dealing with Adolf Hitler himself...and that Milan Meier and Kyla Fluss are part of his plan to establish a renewed Reich based in South America."

They sat there silently for a while, their eyes on the Hitler-esque Von Koerber photos.

Finally Stacey said, "This is madness."

"It always was madness," Sand said, "the Nazi cause. And there are thousands of ex-Nazis in South America right now, and sympathizers not only in South America but the United States. The Free World may presently be in more danger than at the height of the war. A third World War breaking out this close to the US border—even if the atomic threat could be contained—would find the military woefully unprepared, and a pampered populace temperamentally ill-suited. The last two wars were oceans away from the Continental United States. Forget the Cuban missile crisis—this would be on their literal doorsteps."

Charlotte cocked an eyebrow. "If you're right, John, GUILE may be the only thing standing in the way of the Nazis reborn."

Sand nodded. "Without the Global Unit, it would be difficult for the allies to come up with a cohesive response until after some atomic strike—like blowing up the Berlin Wall, as you've speculated, Charlotte. Which is why it's imperative we find that uranium before Meier can turn it into a nuclear weapon."

Frowning, Stacey said, "Surely we need to inform Double M before attempting anything on our own."

Sand thought about that. "Our unfortunate friend Juan Pablo reported hearing of a second shipment of 'material'—almost certainly uranium. 'Ready to set sail.'" He flipped a hand. "There's no time for anything but action."

Charlotte asked, "You have something in mind?"

Sand nodded. "Something offering a slim chance, perhaps, but a chance. If one of us survives, he or she gets word to Double M. If we all turn up dead, that will send a message to Marbury in and of itself."

* * * * * *

They still had all of their armaments from the Pilgrim mission. All they needed from GUILE HQ was a Geiger counter and, armed with that, they headed for the docks, with plenty of freighter piers to check. Millions of metric tons of freight passed through the port of Buenos Aires every year, and that was just the legal goods—never mind the numerous smuggling shipments like the uranium Meier had stolen.

While legal shipping would have printed schedules, smugglers were predictably far less hospitable about sharing sailing timetables. And all that freighter traffic meant hundreds of ships unloading and loading every day. From this array, the Sands and Charlotte had to find one particular ship—a freighter whose name they did not know, and whose departure time was a mystery.

That much traffic also meant hundreds of men working around the area all day and night whose attention the trio would want not to attract. Slinking around the dock areas after dark was dangerous enough when you weren't looking for Nazis smuggling radioactive material.

The night was cool, nearly starless, with only a sliver

of moon providing friendly shadows for the trio to hug; they were in lightweight black sweaters and pants and gum-sole sneakers, faces smudged with black greasepaint, the women in ponytails, holstered sidearms on their hips. There would be no attempt to blend in with anyone or anything but the gloom.

Beyond weapons, the only tool was the Detectron Geiger counter, a gray metal box with a wand and, on top, a dial, controls, and bicycle-style grip. Sand took charge of the gizmo while the other two stayed alert for any sentries posted to protect the precious deadly shipment.

They mostly positioned themselves between the hulking harbor buildings, some of which hummed with activity—refueling, repairs, preparing cargo for transfer. These structures themselves were worth a wave of the Geiger counter wand, but Sand suspected the shipment was already aboard one of the looming freighters.

The needle stubbornly refused to jump as they moved down the first row of ships, ducking between buildings, staying out of streetlight-style illumination. A symphony of sounds underscored their work—the slosh of water, seagulls mewing, bells, horns, clanking chains, industrial hum, sailors laughing, sailors swearing, wooden gangplanks creaking. And yet the overwhelming atmosphere seemed subdued, as if at night this busy harbor were walking in its sleep.

Nothing registered down the whole first row of ships. The second fared no better, although a patrolling security guard livened things up a bit, sending them scurrying back between buildings until he passed. They didn't particularly want to kill anybody, Nazis excluded.

Up and down the rows they went, the process feeling endless, with Sand wondering if this damn gray box even

worked. They were less than two hours from sunup and
heading for their forty-seventh ship when three men drifted
out of a warehouse up ahead—two were seamen, and one
was Milan Meier in a gray, vaguely militaristic topcoat.
Sand steered the women behind a big crate and they all
ducked down, as if bullets were flying, which they weren't.

Yet.

Meier was saying, "You must be out of the harbor before sunup, Schmidt. Else there will be no bonus."

Sand peered around the crate—Meier was addressing
a man in a captain's hat, white in the night, a dark topcoat
over his shoulders, hands out of sight. The other seaman,
the captain's first mate perhaps, wore a stocking cap, a
navy sweater and pants, colors blending with the dark.
But even the darkness was not enough to discourage Meier
from wearing his tinted glasses.

Sand glanced toward the ship, labeled *La Libertad* in
white letters on the bow. No need to confirm it with the
Geiger counter, which might be heard and give them away.

This was the ship, all right.

And us, Sand thought, *with no boarding passes....*

Hunkered down, the two women huddled close to Sand,
whose whisper was barely audible. "Here's what we're
going to do. Charlotte, take out the captain. Stacey, that
first mate is yours. And Milan is mine."

"When?" Charlotte asked.

"On the count of three. Just stand and fire. Zero in on
your assigned target, but don't be fussy."

Stacey gripped his sleeve. "Just kill them? And then
what?"

"Then that ship isn't going anywhere with its captain
and first mate dead, not to mention its prize passenger.
Anyone who comes at us with a gun from that ship is fair

game. When this shakes down, with any luck, we'll be in the custody of the Buenos Aires police."

His wife was doing her best to process all this. "And then what?"

"And then we wait for our daddy to bail us out. Double M looks after his children, you know."

Stacey sucked in a deep breath. She let it out. But then she nodded, on board. Charlotte already was.

Sand smiled at the women and said, "One..."

They were ready to get quickly to their feet.

"Two..."

Pistols drawn.

"And..."

On the deck of the ship above, someone shouted in Spanish, "*Intruders!*"

No need to wait for that last number.

They exploded out from behind the packing crate, as men above rushed about on deck, their three targets sprinting for the freighter's gangplank, Meier in the lead, the captain close after with the first mate right behind.

Sand was taking aim at Meier, half-way up the walkway when the captain turned, a Schmeisser machine gun in his grip, coming out from under that topcoat coat draped over his shoulders. Sand dove to pull Stacey down, Charlotte dropping to the dock, and they rolled as a fusillade chewed up the cement around them, concrete chunks and dust flying like some new weather the devil invented. Then the three were up the gangplank, Sand getting off one wild shot that sparked when it clanged off the steel side of the ship.

On one knee, Charlotte fired repeatedly up toward the deck, forcing the crew to keep their heads down while Sand and Stacey sprinted up the gangplank. They were a little more than halfway when Charlotte stopped firing.

That meant her clip was empty. He started shooting, Stacey following suit toward the aft end as he blasted toward the bow, the shapes of their adversaries just dark masses on the barely lit deck.

Charlotte ran up the gangplank after them, slamming another magazine in as she went. Catching up to them, she yelled, "Down," and they obeyed as she fired again, over their heads, handgun thunder cracking in the night. Still on the gangplank, the couple moved forward but more slowly as they neared the deck.

Sand was in the lead, eyes quick-scanning for threats. Then the captain with the machine gun suddenly rose at the end of the gangplank, the Schmeisser pointed in their direction.

The captain paused momentarily, gritting his teeth, his arm tensing as he apparently weighed whether to murder these would-be passengers or take them into custody. That was as far as he got before Sand put a round in his forehead. The captain went down, not with his ship perhaps, but on its deck.

Then they were on deck, too, but upright. Meier was sprinting aft, two more crewmen with Schmeissers right behind him, running half-turned, their pale white faces smears in the night. The first mate was climbing the stairs to the door of the bridge. Sand took off after Meier while Stacey went after the first mate, Charlotte laying in covering fire from beside the superstructure wall.

As Meier and his two Schmeisser-lugging sailors got near the stern hatchway, one spun and opened fire. Sand was forced to hit the deck; but when the guard had emptied his clip, and turned to follow Meier, Sand shot the guard in the back. The crewman pitched forward onto the steel deck, gun clattering.

Sand was up, ready to chase after Meier and his remaining protector. He was about to reach down for the
fallen (and clearly dead) man's Schmeisser when another
crewman popped out from behind the hatch cover of the
nearest hold and swung a metal pry bar down across Sand's
arm. Sand had barely seen him coming, but dodged enough
to take a glancing blow and not full force, which surely
would have broken his arm.

But the blow was enough to send Sand's Walther flying
and then spinning across the deck, leaving Sand to pirou-
ette and kick the crewman in the face. As the man fell back,
Sand rushed forward, his switchblade snicking open half a
second before it rammed into the crewman's neck. Blood
spray dampened Sand's black sweater, not showing much,
although blood droplets pearled his face. Sand wiped his
eyes free of the blood as the crewman dropped the pry bar
and walked backward a few paces, then sat down hard
on the deck, hands clutching his throat as blood squirted
through his fingers.

Scrambling back across the deck, right arm stinging,
Sand snatched up his Walther and chanced a look forward.
Stacey was pressed to the wall next to the bridge door,
firing at crewmen farther forward. Charlotte was climbing
toward her, both drawing fire.

If he stood here long enough watching them, they would
all three wind end up dead. He went through the nearest
hatchway, then down a flight of narrow stairs to the next
deck where he paused to listen.

* * * * * *

Stacey, her back against the wall of the bridge, tried the hatch
handle—locked. From somewhere aft a bullet clanged off
the steel wall, just overhead. Dropping to a knee, she fixed

her target and fired, just missing, the bullet careening off a hold hatch cover as the crewman dove behind it; but when he came up to fire again, she was ready. Her second shot hit him in the chest, like a punch, toppling him.

Charlotte was firing down the stairs; someone screamed and a body tumbled to the bottom, by which time the screaming had stopped.

Stacey said, "Hatch is locked."

"But of course," Charlotte said. She handed Stacey her pistol. "This is my last clip. Cover me."

Stacey got between Charlotte and the banister, where she could look down and see aft and then turn to see if anyone was coming up from the bow. She shot only when she saw a target. Using the two guns she could keep them relatively safe for a short time—a very short time.

Charlotte pulled off her belt.

"What, going to whip them?" Stacey asked.

"An interesting idea, but I have a better one."

The French agent peeled the backing off her belt, wrapped it around the locked handle.

"Plastique," Charlotte said. She withdrew a lighter, lit the fuse, then pulled Stacey down a few stairs. Stacey handed Charlotte back her pistol. While the fuse burned, they each took out another crewman, then came a small boom, and a modest fireball, followed by the hatch handle dropping harmlessly onto the deck with a *clunk*. The two women scrambled back up, Charlotte jerking open the hatch door and entering first.

She shot two pasty-faced crewmen, then—as Stacey followed her in—Charlotte stepped to the stunned first mate and pressed the barrel of her pistol in his neck. "You will return to the dock, *s'il vous plaît?*"

He shoved her away and went for a pistol in his

waistband.

Charlotte shot him in the chest.

The two women looked at each other as the first mate crumpled to the floor.

"I don't suppose," Charlotte said, "you know how to *naviguer* a freighter?"

* * * * * *

The light was dim down here below deck, the air stale, hot, and thick. Sand found the sudden quiet damn near alarming, then footfalls echoed from the next gangway down. Meier and a crewman were moving from the deck below him to the next one; but he had no clear shot, with no other choice than to follow. As quietly as possible, Sand got to the second deck, peered down, and a crewman stared up at him.

The man fired his Schmeisser up and Sand threw himself back as bullets swarmed through the opening, clanging as they ricocheted off bulkheads and hatchway stairs. Having that crewman almost take him out so unceremoniously got Sand's attention. From a pocket he extracted a grenade left over from their trip to Pilgrim's clinic. He pulled the pin and dropped it through the hole in the deck, heard it clink off the stairwell.

"*Scheiße!*" the crewman shouted.

Damn indeed, Sand thought, diving back as the grenade exploded and a small fireball erupted through the hole.

He let the smoke clear for a few seconds and when he looked down through, the crewman had disappeared. Well, that was probably the man's blood splattered on the bulkhead, and as the Schmeisser lay on the deck, the poor devil was almost certainly dead.

Ears ringing, Sand eased down the gangway to the third deck, careful to avoid all the slick blood on the steps—in this instance, the gum soles were not helpful.

He couldn't hear anything below him, but this corridor had very few doors until you got to the bow of the ship, with holds on either side, except for the upper engine room access. No sign of Meier, but surely the Dutchman could not have run the length of the ship before Sand got down here, especially now that Sand's adversary was carrying a few extra kilos in his newly paunchy body. Meier could have ducked through one of the doors on this deck, but Sand figured the man would have been knocked on his ass by the grenade blast had he done so.

The engines roared to life. That first mate had taken over for the captain, clearly. Time was running out. He didn't know how long it would take the ship to put out to sea, but he knew they needed to stop this goddamned garbage scow soon.

He dropped down the gangway to the fourth and final deck. Meier had to be below somewhere. Before getting to the engine room proper, Sand would have to check two hatches, one on either side, with nooks and crannies here and there; the engine was running, meaning crewmen, so if Meier had gone that way, he wasn't alone anymore.

Sand moved cautiously forward. He checked the shadows, and open niches where equipment was kept. He found no gunmen, but one fire extinguisher and farther on a fire hose. The hot, stale air smelled greasy, glass enclosed bulbs hanging from the low ceiling, spaced several meters apart, providing just enough light for him to slowly move ahead.

The first hatch he came to said *Toilette*. Pistol up and ready, he eased the door open. The tiny, foul-smelling room was empty—life on a ship like this literally stank. He moved to the door marked *Lieferungen*—Supplies. Within were shelves with extra engine parts, lubricants, tools, and not enough space for a man to hide. The ship lurched and he realized they were moving away from the dock.

Hell.

The engine room door's latch was waiting to be opened. He stood there for seconds that felt like minutes, knowing death might wait on the other side. He'd followed the straightest line between two points, but the dispassionate voice in his head that had kept him alive this long advised him not to go in there.

More than one way to skin a cat, he thought, *and more than one way into that engine room....*

He sprinted back the way he'd come, and went up the gangway to the third deck. The ship lurched again, a backward motion now, which meant they were away from the dock. Before long, they would be headed out to sea. He moved judiciously but quickly along the third deck until he reached the hatch marked *Maschinenraum*—Engine Room.

If Meier and/or his flunkies were waiting for him down a deck, they might not expect him to come out on the higher, smaller engine room level, where one man monitored gauges. He went in and a crewman, his back to Sand, was indeed at a panel of gauges as the turbines came alive, thundering as they increased power; still, Sand wasn't sure he could fire the Walther without anyone hearing him. The metal grating that served as a floor revealed no one immediately below—the rest were probably a welcoming party facing the door he'd almost come through.

Time to act.

Sand pistol-whipped the crewman, who went down without a sound, perhaps still alive, although with a blow like that you never knew.

Below, revealed through the metal grating, a single

sailor ran the engine controls. At the mouth of the short, nearby corridor, his back to the controls and the man working them, Meier stood behind two husky goons with pistols facing that door expectantly. Just as he had thought.

Coming down the metal stairs, Sand took them out with shots to the back of the head; each did a sad little dance before crumpling, leaving blood mist and some wall spatter behind.

The crewman at the engine controls reached for a pistol on a nearby table, and almost made it before Sand shot him in the forehead. He fell onto the metal floor on his back, looking shocked to be dead.

Milan Meier already had his hands up as Sand was coming down. The Dutchman was smiling, but the tinted glasses gave his expression a blankness.

"You have me, Mr. Sand," he said. He knotted his hands behind his head. The dead bodies sprawled at his feet didn't seem to faze him. "Congratulations. We should discuss what happens next."

"I think you know what happens next," Sand said, now on the same deck as his enemy.

"I really don't," Meier said, as if he didn't have a care in the world. "You might kill me, you might turn me over to your superiors. Or possibly there's a third option. We might come to some sort of arrangement. I am a man of means, after all."

"You're a Nazi, and you're staging a comeback for Hitler. That limits the options I'm willing to consider."

Meier's smile broadened. "The first time we met I told you I was impressed with your abilities. I did not lie. I have to believe we still can come to a meeting of the minds."

"Not when you are out of yours. You handed my wife to Jake Lonestarr as a prize. That comes with a cost." Sand raised the pistol and Meier's confidence cracked. He was cringing now. Trembling.

The master race just wasn't what it used to be.

"I thought you understood," Meier said, the words tumbling out. "I *knew* you would best that fool Lonestarr. Didn't I deliver him to you, like a prize steer?"

Sand said nothing.

"You know my aims are altruistic," Meier insisted. "I'm a pacifist! This alliance with the Reich, it's just a means to an end. You and your lovely wife are perfectly positioned to help change the future for the betterment of mankind. Atomic energy *is* that future!"

"That's the trouble with the future."

"...What is?"

"You don't have one."

Sand squeezed off a single round.

CHAPTER ELEVEN
ARRIVALS AND DEPARTURES

Sand, after convincing the second mate to see that the freighter got safely moored again, radioed ahead, alerting the Argentine authorities. A mix of Buenos Aires police and *Policía Federal Argentina* agents were waiting at the dock, annoyed about being called out before sunup but ready to take on the task of searching the ship.

Sand informed the police inspector who ordered him put into custody that he was an agent with the Global Unit for International Law Enforcement, of which Argentina was a member nation, and that this was an authorized operation. To which the police inspector replied, "I have never heard of GUILE, señor." A PFA colonel came over, Sand tried again, and the colonel hadn't heard of GUILE either. Whether they were lying or not, Sand couldn't hazard a guess. But it was clear neither man gave a damn either way.

The little three-person raiding team who'd delivered such carnage aboard *La Libertad* were cuffed and deposited in the back of a police car. The second mate was presenting himself and his late captain (and other now deceased crew members) as the victims of a hijacking attempt. According to chain of command, the second mate insisted, that made him captain and he was ready to make do with the remaining crew, and hoping to depart as soon as the bodies were off "his" ship.

Sand understood at once what they were up against. Von Koerber—who he believed was Adolf Hitler himself—had for some time been in charge of the Department of Records in the government of Argentina. For years, "Von Koerber" had been able to change the identities of citizens, records of ships, and a host of other people and things. Why wouldn't a hiding-in-plain-sight Hitler seek such a perfect position for whatever needed covering up?

Von Koerber had likely been well-positioned enough in the governmental hierarchy to wield influence over who else might be appointed to powerful positions. Perhaps an ex-Nazi or a Nazi sympathizer was in charge of the Argentine Naval Prefecture handling all crimes on the water, or the *Policía Federal Argentina*, on hand here, or both. The three GUILE agents could be swept under the proverbial rug and that uranium would be on its way to God-knew-where by lunchtime.

"John," Stacey said, "you have to do something."

She was next to him in the back seat of the police car with Charlotte on the other side of her.

Sand said, "We're a bit outnumbered. Let's hope they honor the arrested-get-a-phone-call custom in Argentina."

"First," Charlotte said, "we will have to make it to the police station alive."

"Fair point," Sand conceded.

They sat for several more minutes, which was not easy with their hands cuffed behind them. What was left of the night was getting painted red and blue by the lights of official vehicles. Then a fast-moving but unlighted vehicle announced itself with an automotive roar before squealing to a stop.

The prisoners looked out Sand's side window at an olive-drab panel truck, out of the back of which men poured, all in unlabeled military fatigues, carrying rifles. From the truck's passenger door stepped a blond man who looked like an older, somewhat weathered Tab Hunter. No fatigues for him, rather a crisp business suit and tie. He was brandishing his ID, as if it were a beacon in a dark night. The commanding nature of his baritone was unmistakable: "Who's in charge here?" Then he repeated it in Spanish: "*Quién está a cargo aquí?*"

Argentine officers scurried to find their leaders, and the Buenos Aires inspector and PFA colonel rushed forward to find out what the belligerent American was shouting about.

Sand allowed himself half a smile.

Stacey frowned in confusion. "Isn't that your friend from our wedding?"

"Phillip Lyman, yes."

"What's he doing here? You said he was a company man!"

"I did. Just not *what* company or for that matter what *kind* of company."

Charlotte, who was wearing the other half of the smile, said to Stacey, "The 'Company,' *mon cher*, is the CIA. I think we have been rescued as in the American westerns. By the Calvary."

"Cavalry," Stacey corrected absently. "Will it work, John?"

"My money is always on Phillip Lyman."

The little group of the CIA man, the plainclothes inspector, and the uniformed colonel gathered close enough for the three in back of the police car to eavesdrop.

"This is a joint CIA/GUILE operation," Lyman said, "and your government is a member of the Global Unit, which means you are interfering with an international law enforcement effort. Release your prisoners now. They are authorized operatives. The man is the agent in charge."

Some defensive indignation came from the PFA colonel who had previously taken charge. Lyman let the man know he would be busted from colonel to corporal by the end of the day if the GUILE agents were not immediately released. Within seconds, the trio was ushered gently from the police car and their cuffs removed.

The colonel came over, face contorted and his dripping sweat finding a home in a bandito mustache. "We are deeply sorry for the inconvenience," he told Sand obsequiously. "Let us know what we can do to assist you. You have my word—we'll obey your orders, sir."

Sand nodded, managing not to smile. "Then I would request that you clear your men and the police away from the crime scene. GUILE has the situation under control."

With a gulp, the colonel nodded. He might have been doing the bidding of corrupt superiors—that was only a guess on Sand's part, however educated a one—but the colonel's apprehension at being the center of an international incident obviously overrode any such considerations.

Within minutes all the Argentine authorities were gone, and Lyman's men had rounded up the remaining ship's crew and their new captain. These sailors wouldn't be sailing anywhere except a detention camp where the CIA could thoroughly interrogate (and likely forget) them.

When Lyman finally made his way over, Sand shook his friend's hand. "How long has the Company been looking out after GUILE's interests?"

"Since Lord Marbury asked me, while I was in the

neighborhood, to give you some backup, should you need it. He thought you just might, and as usual he was right."

Sand said, "How do you know I hadn't already gotten out of those handcuffs and was ready to spring into action?"

"A wild guess. But you don't want to know what might have happened to you and your lady friends if you'd disappeared down into some dank, dark Buenos Aires dungeon."

"I will take your word for it."

An agent in fatigues came over, thin, narrow-faced, with the look of a family doctor approaching family members with bad news.

"Problem?" Lyman asked.

"There's definitely uranium on the ship, sir, but from what we can tell, it only amounts to about half of what we were told to expect."

Not yet dismissing the mournful-faced agent, Lyman gave Sand a look and said, "You don't seem surprised, John."

"I'm not. A man we interviewed at Pilgrim's clinic told me Meier said 'the second shipment' was ready to set sail. So a first shipment had already been made. I think you can logically assume however much is here, a similar amount has already gone."

"Gone where?" Lyman asked.

Sand shrugged. "It may eventually wind up in Berlin, but that's a guess, and even so, there may be another stop or two first."

Lyman nodded toward the agent, dismissing him.

But the agent lingered, saying, "There's something else, sir."

"What is it?" Lyman asked.

"We have the crew rounded up, the survivors, that is."

"Yes. And?"

"Odd thing—five of them appear to not speak Spanish. They respond only to German."

Sand asked, "How are they dressed?"

The agent shrugged. "Like the others—blue work shirts, dungarees. Sailors."

Lyman's eyes met Sand's. "Nazis?"

"Possibly, but not necessarily. Lots of German immigrants in Argentina. Everybody needs work. But it is suggestive."

To the agent, Lyman said, "Are we having our people safely confiscate the uranium 235?"

The mournful man brightened. "We'll have a team equipped for that here before lunch, sir."

"Good work."

The agent went off.

Turning back to Sand, Lyman asked, "What's next for your little *menage a trois?*"

Sand rolled his eyes. "That's not funny, Phil."

"It's a little funny."

After a sigh, Sand said, "We'll be traveling back to Vegas again, to confer with Double M. We've only accomplished half our mission. We need to find the rest of the uranium before it ends up in a bomb somewhere."

"You have a car somewhere handy?"

"We do."

"Then I don't think you're needed here any longer." Some filled body bags were being carted off the ship. "You've done quite enough."

"We stay busy," Sand admitted. "Thank you for helping out, Phillip."

"Well, you helped me too, John."

"How's that?"

The CIA man grinned. "Tell Double M that Uncle Sam

thanks him for the uranium, and should you happen onto any more, we'll happily accept that, too."

Sand grinned back and again they shook hands.

Friendship aside, Lyman was helping himself as well as Sand—adding hundreds of kilos of uranium to the United States' stockpile would be smiled upon by his superiors, including the one in the Oval Office.

Which is why Sand had decided to keep to himself the full nature of his GUILE operation. The first person to hear in depth about what they'd experienced and learned would be Lord Marbury.

* * * * * *

Once again they made the flight from Buenos Aires to Mexico City. In the Continental Hilton's Maya bar, they resumed their table along the wall by the mosaic-and-metal mural of Lake Patzcuaro, with only the bartender and their waitress for company in the time between lunch and when the after-work crowd would come in.

Nursing a red wine while the Sands drank coffee—the couple had put themselves in charge of the party maintaining sobriety this time around—Charlotte said, "We cut off the head of the snake. Perhaps now the body will die."

Letting out *Gauloises* smoke, Sand said, "What makes you think that by removing Meier I chopped off the head?"

The French woman's sky-blue eyes managed to give him a look both languid and alert. "You believe this has been Hitler from the start?"

"The sweep of this thing suggests as much," Sand said. "While Milan Meier was many things, a flunky was not one of them. If not the mastermind in this, he had a great deal of leeway to do as he pleased. The kind a father might give a son."

Frowning in thought, Stacey asked, "You think Meier may have been Hitler's *son?*"

Sand gave a little shrug, gestured with the *Gauloises* in hand. "It's a possibility that's been scratching at the back of my mind. What do you know about Hitler, my darling girl?"

His wife shrugged. "Nothing beyond what we were taught in school. And what we picked up from the newsreels, and cartoons, when we went to the movies."

Her eyes half-lidded but not sleepy, Charlotte said, "There is much you were never taught. We who were fighting him, on our soil? We learn everything we could."

"For instance?" Stacey asked.

Charlotte shrugged. "Did you know Hitler had the half-niece?"

"No."

Sand did. "She was the daughter of Hitler's half-sister Angela—Geli Raubal. Nineteen years younger than Hitler, but from 1925 to 1931, she lived with him. There are rumors, but no real proof, of them having an affair."

After another sip of wine, Charlotte went on. "In 1929, Herr Wolf discover she was involved with his chauffeur. He forced her to end the relationship, then fired the driver."

Stacey shook her head. "I've never heard any of this."

"It's not," Sand admitted, "typical cocktail hour conversation."

"What became of this niece?"

Sand put out his cigarette in a Maya Bar ashtray. "Depends upon who you believe. Hitler was in Nuremberg the day she allegedly shot herself in the chest with his handgun. They'd argued the day before. The authorities ruled it suicide, but some suspected murder."

Charlotte added, "There were rumors she was pregnant. Whether her uncle or the chauffeur? Who can say."

Sand said, "He seems to have gone into a depression after Geli's death, but pulled out of it to get back on track with his work. He had ambitions to pursue, after all. People to see, countries to invade."

"*Oui*," Charlotte said. "And also perhaps because in 1929 he had met a pretty blonde *fräulein*, the assistant of his personal photographer. A teenage girl—like Geli, twenty years younger than he."

Stacey's green eyes were definitely *not* lidded. "Eva Braun."

Sand said, "Yes. But the Braun girl did not become part of his household until '35—timing that's about right for her to have become pregnant if they might've had a child no one knew about...for example, a son whose name was changed to Milan Meier and then Michel Hearn."

Charlotte nodded. "You seem to have given this some thought, *mon ami*."

He shrugged. "It's just theory. But it makes a certain amount of sense. And obviously Geli is a possible mother of Meier's, too, a love child by his own niece...of course, what kind of monster might do that?"

A rhetorical question.

He went on: "Meier and Hearn are the false identities of a man who had no identity anywhere else that we know of. We *do* know of someone in the Department of Records in Argentina, however, in a position to create false identities, should he care enough about the young man to do so."

"Victor Von Koerber," Charlotte said.

"Who we now strongly suspect," Stacey said, "of being Adolf Hitler himself."

Sand twitched a smile. "A thorn by any other name."

* * * * * *

The next day they landed in Vegas just after lunch. As the plane taxied to a stop, the view out Sand's window revealed a Bentley parked on the tarmac, just inside the wire fence. Double M's chauffeur in livery stood near the vehicle, standing at parade rest.

Exiting into a warm afternoon, with the wooden box he'd acquired at Pilgrim's clinic tucked under his arm, Sand helped the women down from the wing of the small plane and was met by the chauffeur, cap in hand. The slender, mustached driver, a man in his fifties, wore a serious, even somber mien.

"Lord Marbury," he said, "would like a word, Mr. Sand."

Sand sent the two women on and trailed the driver to the Bentley, where the back door was opened for him. He slipped in beside Double M, gravely formal in his usual dark, vested Savile Row, making the secret agent feel severely underdressed in a Ban-Lon sports shirt and slacks.

The chauffeur shut them in.

"Sir," Sand said, with an uncertain smile, "certainly filing our report can't be *this* pressing a matter?"

Double M had a cigar between his fingers, lending him a Churchillian look. "You needed to hear this from me, John. You *haven't* had word, I take it?"

"Word of what, sir?"

Double M's expression did something most unusual for him: he sighed. Then said, "President Kennedy has been assassinated."

"...Sir?"

"In Dallas late this morning. A motorcade. Wife at his side. An assassin with a rifle from above, which should have a familiar ring for you."

Sand sat back in the seat, as if something crushing had forced him there. "What do we know?"

Marbury shook his head. "Very little at this early stage. I will share information with you as I receive it. That much I can pledge to you."

Sand's fists clenched themselves.

Double M was saying, "The Dallas police have the apparent shooter, and that he was alone in this already appears to be the party line. But you and I know, Triple Seven, that this is *not* likely the case—not after the attempt you stopped in Berlin."

"You believe the new Reich is behind this?"

A huge shrug. "I believe nothing but the terrible fact that he's been murdered. I might surmise that it has something to do with JFK spearheading the formation of GUILE. But then there's the Bay of Pigs, and his brother's war on the Mafia, and...damnit, John, any number of people wanted him dead."

"Who does the US government think did it?"

Marbury scowled. "If they know anything, they have not deigned to share it with me as yet." The oceanic eyes narrowed at him. "John...do you have a theory as to who might be behind it?"

Sand grunted a non-laugh. "More than a theory. I *know.*"

An untamed eyebrow rose. "Perhaps *you* would deign to share it with me."

"This will tell you," Sand said, and passed Double M the wooden box. Helped him open it and sorted out the files and photos relating to Von Koerber.

The agent waited as Marbury went quickly but thoroughly through the material.

"So this is Von Koerber," Double M said, thoughtfully, "after the cosmetic surgery. He *does* bear a strong resemblance to Der Führer..."

"Not a resemblance," Sand said pointedly. "Von Koerber *is* Adolf Hitler. He's been Hitler all along. This is not about making someone who *isn't* Hitler look *like* Hitler. This is about making the old Hitler look like the *younger* one—so that when he reappears, he seems the same as he did in his prime. Powerful, not decrepit."

Sand filled his boss in on everything that had happened in Buenos Aires from the surveillance to the assault on Pilgrim's clinic. Marbury knew some of it already, having been briefed by the Buenos Aires office, and Lyman had been in touch, as well. But much was new to him.

And Double M had fresh information for Sand.

"If this new Nazi movement—and perhaps Adolf himself—is behind the Kennedy kill," Marbury said, "it may well be their last gasp. There was a slaughter of individuals who have been identified as Nazi war criminals at what had been the Pilgrim clinic. Apparently these 'Shadow People' of yours were waiting with armament they confiscated from the dead. And the Von Koerber estate itself is burned out and abandoned now. As for Milan Meier, you took care of that problem yourself."

"Kyla Fluss is still out there."

Marbury waved that off. "A relatively minor player. A Mata Hari, a second-rate femme fatale."

"Never underestimate the 'weaker' sex, sir. And then there's the rest of that uranium."

Nodding, Marbury said, "And you can be assured we are already working on that, and I will be riding herd on the Americans on the assassination investigation. But your role in this has come to a close, John. And a job well done."

"*What?*"

"The time has once again come for you to return to Texas and resume your normal way of living. Another mission will come along for you and Mrs. Sand soon enough.

But you need to stand down, John. Your feelings for the murdered man leave you compromised."

"I'm not bloody compromised," Sand said tightly. "Jack Kennedy was my friend!"

"Exactly why you are compromised."

Over time, Sand had come to think a cold black stone resided in his chest where his heart should be. And that was fine with him, because it only made him good at his job. Then he'd met Stacey Boldt, and gradually that black stone evolved into a beating heart. But now that his friend had been gunned down, that black stone had resumed its dominance, engulfing not just his chest but his whole being. Somewhere out there was a madman who had killed eight million and so many more, and now another murder was on that madman's list.

A murder that could not, and would not, go unavenged.

He forced himself to assume a reasonable air. "All right, sir. If you don't want me poking into Jack Kennedy's killing, then at least let me stay on this mission. We need to find the rest of the uranium...and Kyla Fluss. All due respect, sir, she's anything but a minor player. With Meier out of the picture, she might well become Herr Wolf's key operative."

Double M's shrug was barely perceptible this time. "You may be right. I have feelers out about her whereabouts. I'm hoping to have something soon. Global Unit agents are searching for her all around the globe."

Sand said, "If Kyla's in Germany—"

"Leave that to us, and go home until we know more. John, I appreciate that Jack Kennedy was a friend. I want you to take some time to grieve. I can arrange for you to attend the State Funeral, if you like."

Sand shook his head. "No. Sir, thank you. But I will honor him...in my own way."

THREE

FROM BERLIN WITH REGARDS
NOVEMBER 1963

CHAPTER TWELVE

BACKSEAT DRIVERS

On the Cessna 310, headed to Houston, Stacey–seated in back with Charlotte—could see her husband's left fist clenching and unclenching.

To the untrained eye, John Sand might seem calm, even relaxed, and certainly self-composed. The latter was actually the case, but not in a good way. From the moment at the airport when he'd shared the news about his dead friend, Stacey noted the tells: the hard eyes; the increased stoicism; the set of his jaw. He was seething, but in that unsettling, bubbling way of lava preparing to erupt.

And she could do nothing to ease his pain, much less his outrage.

She'd seen many sides of her husband since they met four years ago, but this was something new. He had gone stone cold, and the occasional, barely perceptible raising of his eyelids suggested he was calculating his path to revenge.

Only one person might get through to him, no matter what doubts or suspicions Stacey might have of this person.

And to whom else *could* she turn?

She leaned close to Charlotte and whispered in her ear, just enough so to be heard over the engine thrum. "We must help him."

Charlotte's lovely face swiveled to Stacey, the blue eyes half-lidded but completely cold, as cold as John's. "And we will give it to him," she said. "Whatever he needs to finally rid of the world of Herr Wolf."

The two women were so close they might have kissed, but Stacey's frown spoke of an entirely different sort of intimacy. "There are forces here greater even than John Sand," she insisted. "Even with the likes of Charlotte DuBois helping him."

"Is this so?"

"It is. We three have to stay on call, ready to do our part in this mission, as Double M directs. A one-man crusade could easily result in John's death."

A twitch of a knowing smile. "Perhaps you under-estimate him. Perhaps you do not know him as well as you think."

"That may be true. That's why he might listen to reason, coming from you. You've fought side by side. I love him, but you can talk to him as an equal. In this instance, I'm... out of my depth."

They both glanced forward where Sand—a fist still clenching and unclenching—gazed out at the clear sky, though his mind was likely home to storm clouds and lightning flashes.

Still speaking in a murmur barely audible to the nearby Charlotte, Stacey said, "You may be the only other person he's ever let inside."

A small nod came from Charlotte, her eyes cast downward now. Had her lip quivered or had Stacey imagined that?

"I'm begging you," Stacey said.

Charlotte was studying John, her features cloaked in a beautiful blankness; but Stacey knew the French woman still harbored deep feelings for this man, perhaps even remained in love with him. Right now Stacey didn't care about that, her only concern saving John from himself.

Finally Charlotte glanced at Stacey, her nod quick but final. Stacey took the woman's hand and squeezed, receiving momentary pressure in return.

The plane landed in Houston around dinner time. Their man Cuchillo met them with the black Cadillac. They invited their pilot to join them for dinner, but Tom declined—he'd been away from home long enough. The others went to Christie's on Bellaire, a favorite restaurant of the Sands, and a public place that might possibly draw John out of his trance.

As was their habit, Cuchillo joined them at their table, where even the taciturn major domo added more to the conversation than John, who barely touched his usual fourteen-ounce rare ribeye or his Vodka martini, either. The restaurant itself was doing scant business, the death of a President casting a pall that had sent the nation home to crowd around their cathode tubes.

Stacey did her best to keep things amiable if not light, inviting Charlotte to stay over until they heard from Marbury as to the next leg of their mission. The French agent declined—after tonight, she would return to Vegas and wait there.

"You two do not need me for company," Charlotte said.

But John seemed to need no companionship beyond his own dark thoughts. The ride home stayed silent, and as Cuchillo carried in their bags, Stacey took her husband aside and said, "Darling, please don't shut me out."

"Don't talk nonsense," he said, his first words in some time, the tone as sharp as a slap.

She received it the same way and, flushed with hurt and anger, she went quickly up the stairs.

* * * * * *

Sand watched her go but said and did nothing.

Charlotte, suddenly at his side, said, "Are you going after her, *mon cher*?"

"No," he said. "I can see she prefers her own company."

A light laugh. "Can you who have known so many women know so little of this one?"

He frowned at her. "You think I should—"

She took his arm. "I think we should talk, you and I. Two old friends with nothing to hide, *n'est-ce pas*? It is a lovely evening to sit under the stars. Or would you prefer to watch the *télévision* and suffer with the rest of your country's people over the loss of this good man?"

He frowned at her. "You don't think I should go to her?"

"Oh, *absolument*—but *after* we have talked."

He sent Cuchillo off to deposit Charlotte's things in the downstairs guest room, then led her through the house to the patio and outside under the starry Texas sky. A clear blue Texas sky had welcomed John Kennedy just this morning...

They sat at the small table where he often dined with his wife. Her tone lightly conversational, Charlotte asked, "Do you know why I said no to you, John? When you ask me to marry you, in another life?"

He said nothing.

"*That!*" she blurted. "The silence *exaspérante!* The way you pull inside yourself and shut out the rest of your world...even with me *part* of that world!"

He said nothing.

"You close yourself off," she said, "the human part of you. To do the inhuman things you must do in your job. The bad things that must be done for...what is the expression? The greater good."

He said nothing.

"Me," Charlotte said, "you *could* have let in. I live in that world of yours. I understand the terrible things required of you. I feel the same rage as you when you encounter an evil like Herr Wolf...the beasts who make beasts out of us to battle them."

"Where I have to go," he said, finally joining the conversation, "I don't want Stacey to follow."

Her expression was darkly amused. "And where would that be, *mon cher?*"

A corner of his upper lip quivered, unbidden. "If I have to kill one hundred men to get close enough to kill this one man, I will do it. You know what that kind of...carnage... can do to a man's soul."

"Or a woman's."

He nodded. "Or a woman's."

Her gesture was as casual as it was broad. "But Stacey, she has *already* followed you there. She loves you enough to risk all of this..." She waved around to the *Plata Luna* and its grounds. "...to be at your side. To become like you."

"She's not like me."

Charlotte leaned toward him. "John, in Buenos Aires, on that ship of death, she is side by side with me in the fray. She kills men, without remorse. She has joined *your* fight."

A bitter laugh. "What fight is that?"

"Whatever fight is yours."

An ellipsis of night sounds dotted the silence—insects, birds, frogs, wind.

"I've done," he said with a shake of his head, "a terrible thing."

"You have done *many* terrible things, *mon cher.* To what one do you refer?"

"Allowing Stacey into this...this hellish life of mine. That wasn't my intention. I meant to quit and join *her* life, not draw her into mine. How could I have let her train as an agent? Bring her with me on missions, put her in danger? I would never forgive myself if..." He swallowed; looked into the darkness. "...if what I must do now would put her at even *more* risk than I stupidly already have."

The night sounds continued, the wind picking up a bit.

"True," Charlotte said. "The man you seek to avenge had many powerful enemies, this new Reich only one. Gangsters, rogue CIA, Russia, Cuba...even your neighbors, Texas oil men who wanted him dead. But do you think she is not safe at your side? Bring her the rest of the way into your life, John. *Let her in.* You two are one now, or you are nothing, *comprenez-vous?*"

He did not respond, but he knew she was not wrong.

They went back into the house. In the foyer, with its grand staircase, under the garish chandelier Stacey's father had taken such pride in, Sand drew Charlotte close enough for a kiss. But what he bestowed instead was his thanks.

"You are most welcome," Charlotte said with a bitter-sweet smile. "You have a home here, John, and a wonderful woman, beautiful and rich, living the kind of life people in our dark trade never realize. I should hate her. I should hate you both. But I fear the opposite is true."

Cuchillo materialized to show the guest to her room.

Sand went upstairs, finding the door to the master bedroom unlocked, which surprised him.

She was stretched out, still in her clothes, propped by

pillows, arms crossed, a tissue balled in one fist.

"I owe you an apology," he said.

She nodded, barely, a shimmering curtain of tension between them.

He moved through it and sat on the edge of the bed near her. "I won't shut you out again."

"Is that a promise?"

"It is. Conditionally."

Her chin came up. "There are conditions?"

"Just one. If I deem something too dangerous, you will let me handle it alone. I won't hide from you what it is, but in some circumstances, your presence might be enough to...throw me off. And getting us both killed is not a desirable outcome."

"This is Charlotte's advice?"

He shook his head. "No. She would have me ask no conditions. She would have me let you in all the way."

"She loves you, you know."

"She did. But that was a long time ago."

"For you, perhaps." His wife was studying him. "What now?"

His shrug came in slow motion. "Today's tragedy in your home state? What you see is a headline, what you hear is a news bulletin. What I see and hear is that a man I worked for, a man who was my friend, was murdered. I need to address that."

Her nod was in slow motion, as well. "What does Double M say?"

"Marbury wants me to stand down. To await further orders. For all *three* of us to wait for our next orders."

She cocked her head, narrowed her eyes. "That's the extent of it?"

"He said his people, *our* people, are already on the

ground, gathering the facts. That the President's murder would not be taken lightly."

Her short laugh held no humor. "I should think not. Are you going to do as he asks?"

A smaller shrug.

She touched his shoulder. "Come to bed. We'll know better in the morning."

He leaned in and kissed her, gently. "I need to go over some materials first. I may be able to get a bead on where that uranium might be heading. I'll be in my study."

They shared a quick, conciliatory kiss, and he left her there.

* * * * * *

With an oil-painting portrait of Dutch Boldt looking on, Sand sat at his late father-in-law's massive desk in the light of a banker's lamp not unlike Marbury's and went through the files and assorted documents sent along with him by his superior. He pored over reports of ships leaving Buenos Aires, both those on record and others observed by spotters recording comings and goings, then compared those to reports of vessels bound for ports around the globe. This was the kind of tedious work his author friend tended to leave out of his fanciful versions of Sand's cases.

While he felt he was accomplishing something, being at home at all seemed wrong—his place was in Argentina, finding this man he felt sure was Hitler, killing the bastard responsible for the murder of the Free World's leader who just happened to be John Sand's friend.

After around an hour of this, Cuchillo stuck his head in. "Mr. Sand, is there anything further you need of me? The women have retired for the evening."

Sand, lighting up a *Gauloises*, gestured across at a chair

opposite the desk. "Sit for a moment. Would you like to pour us a whiskey first?"

"Why not, sir?"

Cuchillo did so.

They sipped and Sand said, "It's possible at some point, possibly soon, that you may have to step in for me where Mrs. Sand's safety is concerned."

"Always, sir."

"She may wish to follow me into harm's way and I would hope you'd help me to discourage that. She might not be...happy with me."

"Understood."

"It may be necessary for you to remove her from these premises and go to ground. Send any communications to me through Boldt Energy channels. Not here at the house by phone or otherwise."

Cuchillo nodded. Finished his whiskey. "Anything else, Señor Sand?"

Sand rose. "No. Just to offer you my hand."

Which he did. The two men shook.

The *ex-federale* closed the door behind him and Sand returned to the documents.

At just after one in the morning, Sand reached for the phone and woke their pilot.

"Tom," he said, "get the plane ready. Now."

"Yes, sir." The man Sand often referred to as Tom Something, because of a nearly unpronounceable middle-European last name (Rzepczynski), was no longer phased by such sudden requests.

Sand did not return to the bedroom nor did he go to Cuchillo's quarters and wake the man. He simply put on his shoulder rig with his Walther, his ankle holster with the Beretta, and slipped his switchblade into a pocket of his black slacks. He put on a black suit coat over his black Ban-Lon sports shirt to conceal the Walther, then got into a pair of black rubber-soled Italian loafers. The last time he had applied this degree of stealth in his own house had been when he came home to find not an unwanted intruder, but President Kennedy waiting for him here in this study.

Which, after a reflective pause, he now exited.

He walked back around to the garage, got in his British racing-green MG, and eased away from the house, pleased he'd woken neither Stacey nor Charlotte, their bedroom lights still off.

The streets and highways were clear of traffic at this hour, most citizens home sleeping, unsettled by the death of their leader but most likely feeling safe enough in their beds. Had they shared Sand's knowledge of the state of the world—the living, breathing presence of Adolf Hitler in it, perhaps topping the list—they'd be lucky to catch an untroubled nap in the foreseeable future.

He pulled the MG into the Boldt company hangar, empty now, the plane already out on the tarmac being fueled. Sand got out of the car only to find Tom striding toward him, a paper cup of coffee in hand.

"Almost ready to go, boss."

"Thank you, Tom. Sorry about the short notice."

Tom gave him an odd grin. "Getting used to it, Mr. Sand. Go ahead and get on board—I'll be along as soon as I get through the maintenance check list."

Sand opened the door and, as he climbed in, his gut went as tight as a wrung-out washcloth. Sitting in the two back seats were Stacey and Charlotte—alert, poised, their make-up and hair bandbox perfect, beautifully feminine in polo tops and slacks, turquoise and rose respectively.

He climbed in, took the front seat. Looked back at the

two women, nonplussed.

Stacey said, "Cuchillo sends his apologies."

"Perhaps," Sand said, "I should have remembered he raised you from infancy."

"Perhaps," she said. "Also, who signs his paycheck."

Charlotte raised a forefinger. "If the loving reunion is over, might I bring you up to date, Agent Sand?"

"By all means."

"Double M has informed me Kyla Fluss, still traveling as Michelle Rivers, is en route to Berlin. He suggests we intercept her there. Well...it's not really a suggestion."

"I would imagine not," Sand said.

"So," Stacey said, "would you please inform our pilot to reroute us from Mexico City to New York, where we can catch a plane better equipped to fly us to Germany."

"Or," Charlotte said, "or are you too busy trying to avenge your famous friend than to perhaps help save the world?"

"Those goals," he said, matter-of-factly, "may not be mutually exclusive."

The two women exchanged arched-eyebrow expressions.

Tom was climbing into the cockpit. "I hope I'm not interrupting anything..."

Sand said lightly, "No, Tom, not at all. Mrs. Sand and Miss DuBois were just inquiring about our destination. Would you mind telling them where we're bound?"

"New York," he said. "La Guardia...unless you've changed your plans, Mr. Sand."

"I have not."

Charlotte, big blue eyes bigger than ever, asked, "You were *already* intending to fly to Berlin?"

He nodded. "I'm ninety-nine percent certain that's where the uranium is bound. Informed now that the Fluss woman is headed there as well, that makes it one hundred percent...Tom, radio ahead and get us two more seats for the Berlin flight."

"Can do, boss," the pilot said.

Charlotte said, "There's two more things, John."

He returned his attention to the women. "Yes?"

"Hitler and Eva—their blood types? Both were...or I should say *are*...type O. That means any child of theirs would have to be the same. And, Lord Marbury informs me, Milan Meier was type A."

Stacey said glumly, "So much for your theory that Hitler and Meier were father and son."

Tom got them into the air and headed east into the night. As soon as they were airborne, Charlotte said, "Double M had one last new tidbit to share—seems they found a glove-box system in a crate on the ship we stopped."

"Interesting," Sand said.

"*What* kind of system?" Stacey asked.

"A laboratory glove box," her husband said. "You'll be encountering those soon enough on the nuclear side of Boldt Energy—a securely sealed container box with openings on the same or opposite sides with attached gloves...it allows the operator to work inside an isolated environment."

Stacey was processing that as Charlotte said to Sand, "What makes you think the uranium is headed for Berlin?"

They were having to speak up over the engine noise.

"*La Libertad* was bound for Lisbon, Portugal," he said. "The manifest listed the cargo as tractor parts. I just went over records which establish that forty-five days ago the *Desert Night*, a cargo ship of Moroccan registry, left Buenos Aires with a load of tractor parts. The ship was also bound for Lisbon, Portugal, according to the manifest. A record approved by an old friend of ours—Victor Von Koerber."

Charlotte asked, "Where is this ship now?"

"A GUILE agent in Gothenburg, Sweden, saw the *Desert Night* being fueled there a week ago. The agent talked to one of the sailors fueling the ship, who said it was headed to Rostock."

Stacey asked, "Rostock?"

Sand said, "That's in East Germany, the country's eighth largest city, actually."

"No western countries," Charlotte pointed out, "are legally allowed to trade with East Germany."

"Precisely," Sand said. "Which means..."

Stacey said, "The *Desert Night* is smuggling something." He nodded.

"So why," Stacey asked, "are we going to Berlin and not Rostock?"

Charlotte said, "Because the uranium is already gone, is it not, John?"

"That is my supposition," he said. "And I admit that what I have from here on is *mostly* supposition...albeit based on what we know. The ship left Gothenburg a week ago, and—as there's been no news of any sinking—we can safely assume the *Desert Night* made it to Rostock."

Both women nodded.

"My thinking," he went on, "is that if *La Libertad* had a glove-box system aboard, so did the *Desert Night*."

"To what purpose?" Stacey asked.

He raised a cautionary palm, reminding them this was supposition, if fact-based. "When I was on the dock in Buenos Aires with my CIA friend, one of his agents said they found five crewmen on this Argentine ship who spoke only German...only I don't believe they *were* crewmen."

Charlotte asked, "Who were they then?"

"Keep in mind the probable use a glove-box system

has in this context."

Stacey, getting it, said, "Working with radioactive material."

"Yes," Sand said. "What if our five German speakers weren't sailors, but ex-Nazi scientists? And perhaps we can X out the 'ex.' *That* is why we're not bothering to go to Rostock. No offense to the city council and its mayor, but Rostock is simply not worth blowing up."

Charlotte said, "But Berlin...or should I say its wall... *would* be."

"As you theorized," Sand told her. "I believe those scientists built something very special on the trip from Argentina to Rostock. That we're no longer looking for smuggled uranium, but...an atomic bomb."

Stacey's mouth dropped open and she covered it.

Sand said to her, "Remember what Meier said to us the first time we met the man? That all people should have what he had—complete freedom. The people of East Berlin don't have any freedom at all. Perhaps Meier meant to set them free."

His wife blurted, "By blowing them up?"

Sand shrugged. "Some would die, perhaps many—that would depend on the size of the bomb. But even a small atomic device would rip a hell of a hole in the Berlin Wall."

"And," Charlotte said, "quite possibly set off a third World War."

"Since we now know," Sand said, "that Meier was never really in charge, this plan is probably the brainchild of Hitler himself. I can see how, in his twisted mind, it might serve two purposes."

"Such as?" Charlotte asked, as wide-eyed now as Stacey.

"Berlin was to be Hitler's Shangri-La," Sand said, "the perfect city—the citadel on the hill for the whole world to see...a goal the Americans, British, French, and Russians prevented him from achieving. By blowing it up, or even just part of it, he sends a demented 'up yours' message to the lot of them. But there may be genius in the madness—if he can lay the blame at the feet of any one of them, not only will he start World War III, he will make sure that when he steps forward and announces his return, all of Germany will stand in support of his glorious renewed Reich."

CHAPTER THIRTEEN
ROOFTOP DYING

Rolf Schreiber didn't line up with the public's current image of a secret agent, as portrayed in the novels of Sand's ex-colleague, those fanciful reworkings of MI6 reality now appearing on screen in even more outlandish form in international cinemas. Middle-aged, paunchy, hair receding, glasses perched near the tip of his wide, vein-shot nose, Schreiber had the appearance of someone's bachelor uncle who worked as a clerk or accountant.

Which of course was far closer to the typical espionage operatives Sand himself had encountered over the years.

And yet despite such rumpled, unthreatening looks, Schreiber was a first-rate observer, a wily agent with a keen grasp of politics and human nature, blessed with an eidetic memory. An original member of the West German federal intelligence service, the *Bundesnachrichtendienst*, Schreiber had been requested by Double M when GUILE was chartered, the BND somewhat reluctantly allowing the transfer of this valuable agent.

Schreiber, a connoisseur of beer, took a deep swallow of his *Hefeweizen*, then set the pilsner glass on the table and wiped a sleeve across his satisfied grin. Charlotte, seated next to him at Sand's suggestion, averted her eyes; the local GUILE contact was also a connoisseur of beautiful women, if often from a distance.

Sand and Stacey were seated across from the mismatched pair in a booth in a *Kneipe* in Berlin. On this late afternoon, Sand in his gray suit with a black turtleneck was of course far closer to the public's misconception of a secret agent, both women suitable for co-starring roles, though Stacey's cobalt blouse and plaid skirt and Charlotte's navy blue-and-white swing dress were more touristy than chic.

Stacey applied to herself a reasonably believable smile for their unappetizing host as Sand asked, "Rolf, what can you tell us about the woman we're seeking?"

His voice low and raspy, Schreiber said, "Our *falsch* Southern belle, Kyla Fluss, or Michelle Rivers as she presents herself, goes nowhere without her two bodyguards. One is an armed *leibwächter* who has traveled here with her before—she introduces him as Rockwell, her husband."

Sand said, "Rocky Rivers. We've met."

"Most unpleasant man," Schreiber said before taking another sip of beer. After he swallowed and again wiped his chin with his sleeve, he added, "But the second is a German national. He poses as a guide, and is less a gorilla than Rockwell, but he too has a gun...though not a decent tailor. I saw the bulge. For a supposed guide, he is notoriously tight-lipped."

"With a tight-lipped 'guide,'" Sand said, "and a 'husband' who can barely talk, perhaps *you* could fill us in, Rolf...where they might not be so inclined?"

Schreiber chuckled. "John, you are an impatient man."

Pleasantly, Stacey said, "Tell us something we don't

already know."

The chuckling gave way to a cackle. "The 'guide' is Leo Kraus, a German national and suspected professional killer. Slender for a bodyguard, but tall. Bland, no particular distinguishing features. Blue eyes, which do not make him stand out in a German crowd. The taciturn Leo's younger sister, who lives with him, however? She is far more loose-lipped, especially when tight in the *betrunken* sense...and in the throes of passion."

The women gave Schreiber a look. Sand already knew this connoisseur of feminine allure occasionally got lucky.

Casually, pretending not to be proud of himself, Schreiber said, "We operatives all have our methods. This is fresh intelligence, by the way."

Sand asked, "And what did this tight loose lady say?"

"That her brother has an appointment at the Café Kranzler this evening."

Sand frowned. "And you expect Kyla Fluss to be there?"

Schreiber shrugged. "A not unreasonable assumption. Kraus has practically been living with the woman and her 'husband.' What is the American expression? It's worth a shot."

Charlotte asked, "Do you have a time for this meeting?"

"Alas not. In certain situations, the information must flow naturally or not at all. But I do know that Kraus asked his sister if she knew of anyone with a truck to rent."

Sand asked, "And did she?"

"She did not. But she was with her brother Leo when he telephoned two other contacts, and they are the ones he is meeting tonight at the Kranzler. That, I am afraid, is the extent of what I have for you."

"And it's appreciated, Rolf," Sand said. "Thank you."

"Do you wish my assistance this evening? This city is

ever-changing and I do know my way around."

"I'm sure you do, but no. We can take it from here."

The German agent shrugged, finished his beer, then rose and nodded to the little group. "Then I will take my leave."

"When you report to Double M," Sand said, "let him know we should wrap things up here soon."

"I will do so. And I wish you luck tonight. These are dangerous people, John. But, then...so are you."

Schreiber nodded, then lumbered off. They watched him exit the pub, leering at the occasional fetching female as he went.

Then Charlotte said, "I have never worked with this man. You have, John. And you trust him?"

"I do. He's not much to look at, which in this work is to his benefit. Even as he's ignored, he sees everything and everyone else."

Stacey said, "Is it too early to drop by Café Kranzler? We don't have an exact time for the meet."

"We'll go at dusk," Sand said. "Schreiber said 'evening' which should make it soon enough. We'll go back to the hotel, change into things more suitable for night work. While we're there, I'll outline the plan."

Charlotte said, "You *have* a plan?"

"I will."

They made a quick cab ride back to their adjoining rooms at the Savoy Hotel Berlin in the Charlottenburg district, from which they'd only be five and a half kilometers from the Café Kranzler in the Mitte district. In November, Berlin's daily high temperatures hit around five degrees Celsius, getting down to one degree Celsius at night, almost freezing, making walking a less than attractive option.

Sand changed into a dark, heavier-weight suit from Rex's in Houston—Savile Row being possibly inappropriate for the endeavor ahead, the outlines of which were indistinct at this point. Over this he slipped a lightweight black overcoat, wanting nothing cumbersome in case of trouble. His Walther nestled in his shoulder rig, the Beretta in its ankle holster, switchblade in an overcoat pocket.

He gathered the two women and gave them a rundown. His intention was to stay on the street outside the Café Kranzler and do his best to grab Kyla before she and her gunmen even made it inside. Charlotte was now in an insulated black catsuit fitted with several knives and a hip-holstered handgun hidden by a stylish dark gray thigh-length lightweight coat, dark colors that would blend well with the night. She would be their rover, and provide any backup Sand needed.

Stacey wore black slacks and blouse and lightweight topcoat, a Walther tucked under her arm, as well. As the least experienced of the trio, she'd be inside the café, at an out-of-the-way table where she could keep an eye on the main floor. Her job would be to observe Kyla and her bodyguards, should they make it inside, perhaps by a rear entrance or in some other fashion unobserved by the others. In that case, Stacey would watch Kyla and her party and, when they were getting ready to leave, go outside and warn Sand (and Charlotte, too, if she were in sight).

Nothing fancy as plans went, but—with just the three of them—anything more complex might only serve to cause itself problems. Perhaps he should have brought Schreiber in as a fourth, but Rolf was an intelligence-gatherer, not a man of action. And one more player would not solve the logistical challenges the Café Kranzler provided.

Plopped on the corner of *Unter den Linden* and *Frie-drichstraße*, the rectangular, mostly glass-walled restau-rant—three floors of bars and tables—seemed to be crowded at all hours. Thank God the cold kept the sidewalk seating empty this time of year.

Even so, the Kranzler could not be properly covered without at least a team of ten—past what GUILE at this early stage could provide, and a group that size not used to working together was a recipe for disaster. Better a small strike force, with the best outcome grabbing Kyla and her cronies outside the café, whether coming or going.

When they neared the Kranzler—its wide red-and-white striped awnings giving it the look of a permanent circus minus only the animals and clowns—the two women waited outside while Sand went in for a quick walk-through of all three floors. He had described Kyla and Rocky Rivers, and they'd both seen photos of Kyla's transformation from Dr. Pilgrim's files; but as the only one who'd seen Kyla and her faux-hubby in person, Sand needed to make the preliminary recon himself. And even he didn't know what Schreiber's German national looked like—blue eyes. There was a help! All they knew was this reported assassin would likely show up with Kyla.

Sand rejoined the women on the street a block or so from the café.

"It's clear," he said. To Stacey: "There's a good open spot by the windows on the street, and not far from the door on the first floor, where you'll be able to see everyone who enters."

His wife nodded. She didn't look at all afraid, and he loved her for it; but she also didn't seem over-confident, and he loved her for that, too.

Charlotte pointed to a storefront on the opposite corner. "You'll be able to see me there, *mon amis*, and I will be able to see the Fluss bitch and her crew, if they approach on foot from that direction."

"Good," Sand said.

Charlotte took off, falling in behind a group of pedestrians headed that way, then slipped in among them. Within seconds she was invisible.

To Stacey, he said, "These people are lethal. If they get past Charlotte and me somehow, do not...I repeat do *not*... try to take them yourself."

She cocked her head. "The two men don't know me, and the meeting with Kyla was fleeting, last year. I have a certain advantage."

"Perhaps," he said. "But you are a public figure and she has reason to stay informed about the two of us."

"True."

"And these are professional killers, and I include Kyla. You're good, very good. But they have been at this longer, and are better. Wait for us—the three of us will take them together...I'll be tucked in that doorway." He indicated where.

She nodded. Businesslike.

Then he gave her a quick kiss on her pretty mouth, not at all businesslike.

"I love you," he told her. "Now let's get to work."

* * * * * *

Stacey had felt butterflies in her stomach only twice before in her life. Once in the tenth grade, in the wings, before going on stage as the lead in *Annie Get Your Gun.* She had done just fine, and in subsequent high school and college productions of *Oklahoma* and *The Unsinkable Molly Brown,* she had not felt nervous at all.

The other time had been her first day as executive vice president of Boldt Oil, the only female on the top floor but for secretaries, all those men wondering if she was as good as her daddy said she was...or would any little rich girl with a business degree get the same break as long as she was Dutch Boldt's daughter?

The third time for butterflies came as she strode to the front doors of the Café Kranzler. She wanted to make John proud, but was she ready?

She strolled into the noisy, smoky lobby of the café, greeted by an attractive dark-haired woman in a navy-blue hostess dress with white piping. "*Guten abend, wie viele heute abend?*"

"I'm sorry," Stacey said. "*Ich spreche kein deutsch.*"

I don't speak German.

The hostess smiled. "Good evening—how many in your party?"

"I'm expecting three others," Stacey said. Not exactly a lie.

"Could your party already be here, *fraulein*?"

Stacey shook her head. "I'm afraid I'm terribly early. I didn't want to be late, and this city..." She shrugged, provided an embarrassed smile. "...I get turned around so easily."

Her patience starting to fray, the hostess asked, "Would you like to wait at the bar?"

Stacey indicated an empty table with four chairs near the front window and in sight of the door, clearly the spot John had recommended. "Might I wait for my party there? Where I can see them come in?"

"Quite so," the hostess said.

Through the bustling, rather noisy dining room, Stacey was led to the table, provided a menu, and told, "Katrina will be your waitress. She will be over soon."

"Thank you," Stacey said, thinking that had been her best performance since playing Molly Brown.

The restaurant was at perhaps half-capacity, the diners boisterous and the hum of conversation coming down through the open well of a rather wide, modernistic spiral staircase.

From her window, she couldn't see John, ducked in his doorway, but could just make out the Frenchwoman standing near the storefront across the street. Charlotte would check her watch, tapping her right foot impatiently, looking off to one side irritatedly—a nice way to keep from appearing to be a streetwalker.

Katrina, a smiling blonde in the same navy with white-piping uniform as the hostess but adding a waitress cap, arrived to ask if she could bring Stacey a drink while waiting for her party. A glass of white wine was ordered, soon arrived, and was sipped by Stacey, whose butterflies had receded though she remained on edge.

Her eyes began a journey—entryway/lobby, window on the street, restaurant main floor—that she repeated again and again. She made the wine last and it did serve to help knock back any jitters, though she determined to keep it to a single glass. Perhaps the longest fifteen minutes of her life passed before her spot at the window revealed a black Mercedes pulling up right in front of her, separated only by the restaurant itself and the sidewalk.

Though she had only seen the woman briefly—and under duress—she knew Kyla Fluss at once, stepping from the Mercedes with an admirably shapely leg extended. Kyla was blonde again and in a black leather catsuit not unlike Charlotte's, apparently the same attire the Fluss woman had worn at the hunting lodge on Curaçao. No topcoat, despite the cold.

Emotions spiked in Stacey—anger, excitement, and (she would not lie to herself) fear.

Two men piled out after Kyla, a burly broad-shouldered one and a slender tall one, both in sharp dark suits. John had positioned himself on the other side of the building, too far around the corner to see Kyla stride across the sidewalk to the front doors.

Across the way, Charlotte was stepping off the sidewalk into the street, dodging traffic, earning honks. Kyla's head snapped around.

The blonde shouted something harsh in German as Charlotte advanced like a western gunfighter, brushing aside her unbuttoned sports jacket for unfettered access to the pistol on her hip. The two men opened fire, whipcracks in the night, bullets dinging into parked cars parked along the street, one a Volkswagen that Charlotte ducked behind, her pistol responding in kind.

On the street, cars sped up or slammed to a stop, screeching tires, bumping bumpers, lanes ignored, the sparse pedestrian traffic scattering, on the run or diving for cover.

Stacey, who observed all this as if on a TV or movie screen, got to her feet. On the far side of the café, the windows revealed John, Walther in his right fist, a blur running by.

Someone in the café screamed, apparently a diner who saw the burly bodyguard charging toward the entry doors before he barreled through the lobby and inside the dining room, a revolver in hand, Kyla on his heels, trailed by the taller bodyguard, wielding an automatic, pausing at the half-open door to fire back, twice, at Charlotte, gunfire and shattering glass making terrible dissonant music. Then he sprinted inside, as well.

"Upstairs!" Kyla shouted, and the burly bodyguard clambered up the brass-and-marble spiral staircase, the blonde in the black catsuit winding right behind him—she had a small revolver in hand herself, yanked from a shoulder-slung purse. Finally the tall bodyguard and his gun caught up with them, rushing to join the violent parade twisting up the stairs.

Already on her feet, Stacey yanked her pistol from under her jacket and ran into the aisle, where she collided with Katrina, bringing an unrequested second glass of wine.

The wine glass and tray flew one way, Katrina tumbled the other, tangling up with Stacey, both women crashing to the floor. Stacey got to her feet just in time to see John sprinting up the spiral staircase, like a corkscrew removing itself; two heartbeats later, Charlotte entered the restaurant and took the same path to the second floor.

Stacey disengaged from the waitress, other diners standing now, with only a few still hiding under tables, the majority milling about, though many clinging to each other. Then came gunfire from upstairs and everyone ducked back down.

A woman's shriek, not the gunfire upstairs, initiated the exodus: customers swimming through each other, making for the front doors, Stacey barely getting out of their path, hugging the window out of which she'd kept watch.

Katrina was getting to her feet, looking more confused than scared. Stacey gestured with her pistol and, needing no further encouragement, the waitress sprinted toward the back and disappeared through double doors into the kitchen.

Stacey was now the sole remaining human standing on the restaurant's main floor, those who hadn't yet fled still cowering under linen-covered tables, the window on the street confirming the disappearance of the Mercedes and its driver. Cautiously, she made her way to the spiral staircase and climbed to the second floor, fanning the pistol around in search of adversaries but seeing only another room of diners cowering under tables and a bar seemingly unattended. One man on his knees beneath a nearby table, his arm draped around his female companion, pointed up to the third floor.

She acknowledged that with a nod, then crouched and pointed the Walther up the well of another brass-and-marble spiral staircase. Nothing up there but a curved ceiling. She was about to start up when more gunshots rang out, oddly muffled...not from a single weapon or from just one area above, either—an exchange of rounds!

Then silence.

Walther at the ready, she went up quick but no less cautious, coming into a circular room, smaller than the other floors, perched on the roof like a flying saucer. The furnishings were white wrought-iron, the effect an art moderne patio, a coffee and dessert area, the customers terrified and tucked under the small round tables, a pie-and-pastry counter seemingly unattended. To her right, a door was open onto the roof. Judging by the muffled shots she'd heard, the fight had moved outside.

"Stay down!" Stacey advised the diners as she crossed the room quickly, stepped out onto the roof, but saw no one. Where could they be? Why had the gunfire stopped?

The enclosed central circular coffee shop only took up perhaps a third of the flat rooftop. Two spent shell casings winked at her from the rubberized surface; she crouched to check them out and realized the rooftop coffee shop—The Barn, as it was called—was raised to provide a crawlspace, an area cloaked in darkness by shadow and night.

Staying low, she slowly circled The Barn, splitting the difference between the rectangular roof and the circular crawlspace to avoid any unpleasant surprises. Her breath preceded her in ghostly puffs, but the cold made no impression upon her. As she rounded the saucer-shaped structure, she came upon a figure standing over a body.

A female figure.

A male body.

Charlotte, pistol in her hand, stood with her back to Stacey. Smoke trailed from the gun barrel as if the downwardly held weapon, too, were breathing visibly in the chill.

John lay sprawled at Charlotte's feet, face down, a small scorched hole in the back of his overcoat. Immobile. Unconscious, or...?

The fallen man's wife said, "*What the hell have you done?*"

Turning toward Stacey Sand, who aimed a gun at her, Charlotte reflexively brought her weapon up as well, the two women and their pistols facing each other.

"We were ambushed," Charlotte said, her voice small and soft in the night. Apologetic, even ashamed.

"He was shot in the back," Stacey said through her teeth. "You were *behind* him."

Charlotte shook her head, the brown tresses flowing in the raw breeze. "John was ahead of me, yes. But someone got between us. Hid under this little round building. And I *shoot* the attacker! See for yourself!"

But Stacey was not about to take her eyes off this traitorous woman—what, believe her lie?

And die?

"People in your company make a bad habit," Stacey said coldly, eyes welling, "of getting ambushed...and shot in the back. Just ask our late friend Jaime."

Charlotte, with her free hand, gestured to John on the

rooftop floor. "I would not kill this man. Before you ever even *knew* him, I love him."

"And now that you can't have him, you're making sure no one else can."

She was shaking her head, frustrated, tears spilling. "I tell you, I shot the man who shot John! He's right over there in the crawlspace!"

Stacey was back in Hogan's Alley in the neon graveyard. Where someone wore a GUILE windbreaker...but also the face of an assassin. And she was not about to fail again... not for herself...not for John....

Charlotte lowered her gun a few inches. "Please, *mon ami*. This does not have to end this way."

"Doesn't it?"

Stacey's shot rattled the nearby glass windows and echoed in the canyon between buildings while blood splashed on the rooftop and tears froze on faces.

CHAPTER FOURTEEN
FAMILY MATTERS

A nearby gunshot woke him with a start, his ears ringing, a pain in his back spreading like spilled liquid under the skin. His eyes opened and a beautiful face was hovering near, green eyes wide, mouth an "O" of surprise.

Not just any beautiful face, but his wife's—Stacey's lovely features framed in the auburn of her hair, fluffed by a chill whisper of wind.

"You're alive!" she blurted.

"So," Sand managed, "it would seem."

She helped him into a sitting position, legs stretching out before him. His back hurt no worse than if he'd been clubbed with a cricket bat.

Then another beautiful female face floated near, as Charlotte crouched and touched his shoulder.

"You are *not* dead, *mon cher!*"

"Must I...I repeat myself?" He blinked at the night, the lights of Berlin flickering like fireflies before him. "I heard a shot, close by...what...?"

Stacey, kneeling next to him, pointed her forefinger past him, indicating a prone figure, barely visible at the edge of the shadowed crawlspace under the circular coffee shop that sat on the building's rooftop like a jaunty cap.

Nothing jaunty about the corpse, however, a tall skinny man in a dark suit with a revolver in his limp fingers, face down, a ragged bloody exit wound in the back of his head.

"Whose delicate work," he inquired, "is that?"

"Mine," Stacey said, rather shyly. "I finally took your advice about head shots...but only because his head was about all I could see."

Both women, at his urging, helped him to his feet. "Bring me up to date, if you would," he said. "Where is the Fluss woman and her 'husband'—this dead man would appear to be Leo Kraus."

"*Oui,*" Charlotte said. "The other two, they ride the awnings down to that Mercedes, which come back for them." She shrugged. "I couldn't risk a shot because too many civilians were here and there."

"Pesky annoyance, civilians," he said, as they provided space for him to climb his grimacing way out of his topcoat and then yank up his shirt above his chest, to reveal—by way of explanation, re: his survival—the green M-1951 bullet-resistant vest he'd added to his ensemble at the last minute.

"Fiber-reinforced aluminum and nylon," he said to them with a smile. "Not exactly slimming, but useful wardrobe nonetheless... Glad to see you girls working so well together."

"Why," Charlotte asked, "would you think otherwise?"

The French agent's eyes met Stacey's and the two women went to each other and embraced. They were whispering to each other, but Sand couldn't make any of it out over the sing-song two-tones of claxons signaling the *Landespolizei* on its way...and judging by the building volume, not far off.

"There's a time and place for everything," Sand said to the women, who were facing each other in a loose embrace, "but this isn't the time for that."

With his ribs hurting, Sand quickly discarded the notion of using the awnings for an escape route. But a peek over the side revealed the daring it had taken to jump from here to the second-floor awning, in hopes it would hold, then doing the same again, and making a hard landing on the street. That level of desperation gave him pause—if Kyla and Rocky Rivers would jump off a three-story roof to avoid capture, surrender for either, in any situation, seemed unlikely.

Instead, after Sand got back into his bullet-torn topcoat, they made their expeditious way down the spiral staircases past two floors of a restaurant still stunned by chaotic events. They were just stepping onto the street when coming into view were the flashing lights of the first oncoming police car, droning its ear-bursting two-note song. Calmly the trio walked away and made a turn into an alley. Only then did they run, sprinting half a dozen blocks before Sand slowed himself and the others to a walk.

Half a dozen blocks later they cut down a side-street sidewalk, then strolled in the direction of their hotel, breaths smoking in the cold. The three of them walked arm in arm, Sand in the center, just another group of friends out for the evening. Or perhaps one very lucky man who'd made two new acquaintances.

They walked the five kilometers or so all the way back to the Savoy, briskly. No chatting among this pleasant company, just the chattering of teeth. Taxis slowed only to get waved along. Even on an increasingly frigid night like this, Sand preferred not to risk giving a cabbie something to remember should inquisitive police come round.

Rather than go immediately to their rooms, they repaired to the lobby's Times Bar with its central, octagon-shaped pillar of clocks reporting the time in major cities around the world. They sat soaking up warmth and delicious coffee at a small round table in the masculine wood-paneled setting where the smell of Cuban cigars (on special license from Castro's government) could not help but make Sand recall the cigars he'd shared with a certain late friend.

Sand said, "I think we bollixed up Kyla's meeting this evening. And my sweet wife here killed Kraus, the bitch's Berlin contact. So maybe we've at least slowed her down a bit. Still, one has to wonder—what might *Fräulein* Fluss be up to next?"

"Something," Charlotte said, "that requires the use of a truck. To transport an atomic bomb, perhaps? If so, from where to where?"

Stacey, over the lip of her coffee cup, pondered aloud: "Could Kyla be trying to move the device from the country into the city?"

"Possibly," Sand said, "but I think not. Rostock is East Germany, after all—the Russians hated Hitler in '45 and I'm confident they still hate him now. Stowing it there would not be a desirable option. The best way for Kyla to deal with this bomb we've conjured is to have taken it directly from the Rostock pier here to the city."

"You believe," Charlotte said, "it is already in Berlin?"

"Yes, somewhere in Berlin with enough privacy to keep it hidden, but near enough to the desired target to make moving it into position less than a huge risk."

Stacey frowned. "French, British, and American armies, GUILE agents...Kyla surely knows any or all of them could be looking for the bomb by now. Where can she be keeping it?"

Charlotte said, "Depends on the size of the thing. How *grosse* do you suppose it is?"

"It would be smaller," Sand said, "than the American atomic bombs dropped on Japan—Kyla has less uranium-235 to play with. But the two American bombs weighed over seven-hundred stone each."

"In American, dear," Stacey said.

"Ten thousand pounds, give or take. So even at a quarter of that amount, you're looking at over a hundred-forty stone—that's a ton to you, darling. With enough yield to destroy a good share of Berlin."

"She would need," Stacey said, "a small crane or forklift to get it out of the truck."

Charlotte nodded. "And she would need somewhere with this kind of equipment. That narrows the search. What else?"

"With that much bulk," Sand said, "you would prefer to be near your target."

"Most of the factories in Berlin," Charlotte observed, "were bombed during the war—some have bounced back, but there are fewer to check, especially those near the wall...if you still accept that as the probable target."

"Meat packing houses," Stacey said, eyes narrowed. "They use forklifts and cranes. Cows and pigs are heavy."

Sand smiled, proud of her. "We will add meat packing houses to the list," he said. "You are thinking, my dear."

"You don't have to sound surprised about it," she pointed out lightly. "Men get themselves into trouble, underestimating women."

"Such true words," Charlotte said.

Sand leaned forward, his jaw dropping. He had complimented his wife for thinking, and now suddenly he had started to.

Slowly he began, "We were operating under the assumption that Milan Meier was the son of Adolf Hitler...a leap we admittedly should not, perhaps, have made. Meier might have simply been a wealthy fascist devoted to bringing Herr Wolf back into power, who'd been put in charge of this key move in the Reich's return from the ashes. But *Kyla Fluss* is in charge now—a woman. Germans answering to a woman. *Why?*"

Stacey asked, "Could she and Milan have been married? Their association seems to go way back."

He flipped a hand. "Even so, what justifies her importance? And what makes Kyla Fluss so determined to carry out this mission that she would jump off the roof of the Café Kranzler?"

"What if," Charlotte said, obviously just thinking out loud, "Meier was Hitler's son-in-law?"

"Meaning..." Sand could hardly get it out. "...Kyla Fluss is Hitler's daughter?"

"Which would make her mama," Stacey said, with a smile that struck Sand as slightly demented, "Eva Braun."

Sand said to the waitress, "Check please!"

* * * * * *

They took the stairs instead of a Savoy elevator and made sure no one was in the corridor of their floor before going directly to their adjoining rooms. Charlotte spoke of craving a shower and Sand asked her to join them after, as he intended to call down for a late dinner for three and a bottle of *Moselle Auslese*. The French agent ducked into her room, and he and Stacey went into theirs.

As soon as he'd phoned in the room service order, Stacey folded herself into his arms and gave him a long, slow kiss on the mouth.

"What did I do," he inquired gently, "to deserve that?"

"I almost lost you," she whispered, fiddling with his hair. She sighed, and her smile had sadness in it. "I don't know if I'm up to this."

"This mission specifically, or the spy life generally?"

"Either one. Both."

He nuzzled her neck, then said, "If you want to quit, that's fine, and I'll join you in your Texas millions, or is it billions? But not until this job is done. I need you, Stacey. Your help. Your brains, your bravery, your heart."

She was smiling at this rare outburst. "All right, then...I'll stay on *this* job, at least. But, John—one question?"

"Yes?"

Her forehead frowned and her mouth smiled. "Did you make it with Hitler's daughter?"

He said nothing for a moment, then: "I'm afraid that's classified."

She laughed. Perhaps with a touch of hysteria in it, but she laughed, and they kissed again.

"Now what?" she asked suggestively.

"A shower."

"Together?"

He tapped her cute nose. "One at a time. You know very well that two-in-a-shower is overrated. Anyway, somebody has to be here when room service arrives."

"All right. Give the man a generous tip."

"Certainly."

"But take your gun along."

"Always."

Room service arrived, received its tip, and left its cart, with no gunplay required. Sand arranged a table for himself, Stacey and Charlotte; he left the serving tray lids on.

When Stacey returned in a white terry robe, her auburn hair in a matching towel turban, he poured her a glass of wine and set off for his turn in the shower.

He let the hot water have at the sore spot on his back where the bullet-resistant vest had likely saved his life.

Giving in to relaxation, however, remained impossible. He could not halt his mind's march through what he knew about Adolf Hitler—from extermination of those deemed inferior to a belief in the supernatural, from Blitzkrieg attacks to delusional dreams of a super army—all were clues to what fueled the master-race mastermind's madness.

Then, suddenly, under the shower's hot needles, he opened his eyes wide.

What if—only eighteen days after eliminating the leader of the Free World by assassination—Hitler meant to detonate his Berlin bomb on December 11, launching his renewed Reich twenty-two years to the day after first declaring war on the United States?

The sick symmetry of the gesture might well appeal to that warmongering maniac. Did that define the time left for GUILE to stop him? A little over two weeks? Still, that meant a hell of a counter-effort could be undertaken. But Kyla Fluss seemed to be on a more accelerated agenda, working to get her bomb in position right now.

Why?

Perhaps Sand and his two female GUILE agents were the answer. The timetable had moved up because of what the trio had uncovered and disrupted in the mountains and on the dock in Argentina. And Kyla was accelerating her plan now that Sand and the two women were closing in.

But were they?

The reality of a bomb seemed well-established, but beyond Berlin itself, Sand had no bead on where in the city it might be headed, other than perhaps somewhere along the wall.

By the time he turned off the water, his back was hurting less but his brain was still spinning. Over his shoulder in the mirror, he checked the blossoming bruise, decided he hadn't broken a rib after all, dried himself off, gave his hair a quick dry with a towel, then wrapped it around his waist and went out into the suite, trailed by steam.

In her white terrycloth robe, Stacey sat on the bed, propped with pillows against the headboard, paging through the Savoy's in-house magazine, her robe carelessly belted and exposing about half of either generous, rounded breast. Charlotte, similarly robed, the slope of her back rising nicely to her plump bottom, her bare legs bent at the knees, feet crossed at the ankles, lay on her tummy reading *Stern Magazine*, which had a sexily smiling Senta Berger on the cover.

Suddenly his mind wasn't spinning. Just reeling. He was either the luckiest man in the world or the unluckiest.

The two women looked up at him, idly, and then both began to giggle like schoolgirls.

"You need a bigger towel," Stacey said.

Their giggling built to genuine laughter.

"Nothing," he commented drily, "you haven't seen before."

Then he padded over to the table and the covered dishes on the cart. The women had already helped themselves to wiener schnitzel and fried potatoes, and—famished—he followed suit. As he ate, he shared with them his shower-stall thoughts regarding Hitler's goals and Kyla's means.

Soon the two beauties had joined him at the table. They sipped wine and nibbled German Spritz cookies as they listened and occasionally questioned. His towel did not come up.

"The longer Kyla waits," Sand said, "the more time we have to convince our superiors of just how major a threat she poses, meaning army detachments and bomb squads mounting the kind of all-out search she desperately wants to avoid. And yet, as we said earlier, she still needs somewhere with access to a forklift or crane."

Stacey said, "And you agree with Charlotte that the wall is the likely target?"

"I do," Sand said, nodding. He poured himself a fresh glass of wine. "Destroy the wall and unite Germany behind the new Reich. That's been the goal from the beginning."

That pleased Charlotte, who was chewing a cookie. "At least," she said, and swallowed, "that gives us a starting point."

"Yes," Sand said pleasantly. "A *twenty-seven-mile* starting point."

Both women frowned.

"Twenty-seven miles," he went on, "of barbed wire, attack dogs, and land mines."

Charlotte, her brow furrowed, asked, "But is that a bad thing for us? Does this not limit where the Fluss *putain* can place her damn bomb?"

He had been lifting a bite of fried potatoes to his lips, but the fork froze in midair. Then he put it down. Looked from Stacey to Charlotte and back again.

"I *know* where the bomb is," Sand said.

CHAPTER FIFTEEN

BLONDE BOMBSHELL

At the table in the Sands' suite, dishes set aside on the cart, glasses of wine poured all around, Sand in his sarong of a towel with the two women in their terry robes and towel turbans discussed the atomic bomb secreted somewhere in the city.

Sand said, "This is about more than just setting off the bomb."

"Is that not," Charlotte asked, "enough, *mon cher*?"

"One might think," Sand admitted. He sipped wine. "But they must lay blame for the bomb and the damage it does on the Allies—the French, the British, the Americans, or some combination...perhaps all three. *That* is how the resurrected Adolf Hitler intends to reunite Germany."

Stacey's eyes were wide and horrified. "By killing his own countrymen?"

Sand shrugged. "Herr Wolf has never been averse to sacrificing his people. Yes, many will die, but he undoubtedly sees that as a necessary sacrifice in turning popular opinion here to his renewed Reich."

Charlotte, frowning in thought, asked, "Why not lay

this horror at the feet of the Russians?"

He waved that off. "The Germans despise the Russians already. Setting east Germans free will galvanize them, while blaming the Allies for the atrocity would woo back west Germans under the evil spell of the Allies."

Stacey gave her husband a puckered kiss of a smile. "As impressive as your analysis of the situation might be, John, would you mind getting around to telling us where you think they've put your goddamn *bomb?*"

He poured everyone more wine.

"Glad to," he said. "Four years ago—not long before we met, my love—I was held prisoner in the tunnels below Tiergarten Park...the *führerbunker*. You may recall hearing of this from me. I was a guest of Crow Nocano, who you may also recall was an associate of Milan Meier's ally, Jake Lonestarr. That...the nest of bunkers below the city, under the wall...is the logical place for Kyla Fluss to plant her bomb."

With a doubtful little shake of her head, Charlotte said, "Those tunnels, they are closed off, long ago."

"Ways in and out remain—I exited through one when I took my leave. Four years ago, it was a semi-abandoned underground city, still home to forklifts for unloading supplies from trucks. That it's been long since sealed off is a widely held, and inaccurate, belief. By the time anyone might think to search those catacombs, it will be too late."

Charlotte said, "*You* have thought to search it."

"I have, and that's why we must act quickly—Kyla knows we are, at least to some degree, onto her plans. And don't ignore the evil poetry of these Nazis, old and new, using the place where Adolf Hitler staged his phony death as the launching pad for his resurrected Reich...and the very real deaths of tens of thousands."

"John," Charlotte said, "I know, *mon ami*, you are thinking that the need to act, the time to act, it is now. But we should call for help."

"If we do this," Stacey said, "we need back-up."

Sand shrugged. "Here are our options—a transatlantic call to Double M over an unsecured phone line—anyone like that? How about calling in Rolf Schreiber? You've seen him—he's the best GUILE agent of the handful in Berlin, a crackerjack intel gatherer but nothing more. Is *that* who you want watching your back?"

"American troops are stationed in West Berlin," Charlotte said, stating the obvious. "Why not call *them* in?"

"We have no liaison at US Army Headquarters," Sand said. "No one designated or cleared for contact. And would we even be believed with such a wild story? It might get us taken into custody."

"That," Charlotte admitted, with a lifted eyebrow, "would not be a good outcome."

"And if Little Miss Hitler smells the army," Sand said, "she'll detonate her bomb then and there, and people will die. A lot of people, us included."

Stacy frowned. "Is there any way to get word to Lord Marbury?"

"I can and will send a coded message through Schreiber in the Berlin office, on our room's obviously unsecure phone line...so even in code it will have to be somewhat elliptical, and a response will take time. And we can't wait for that—we must act and act now."

Stacey stood, took off the turban, shook her hair free. "Then it's up to our little merry band, isn't it?"

Sand touched her arm. "I would say so, my darling girl."

"I have only one question."

"Yes?"

"Just how in hell are we going to do it?"

He shrugged, sending his eyes to Charlotte and back to his wife. "How did we approach Pilgrim's clinic?"

"We didn't 'approach' it," Stacey said. "We went right at them."

Sand nodded. "Indeed so. Of course, the clinic was out in the open. This is an underground lair."

"I hate the underground lairs," Charlotte said with a shiver.

He said, "We go in the way in I already know of, hope it hasn't been blocked, shoot anyone who gets in our way, and secure the bomb."

"If it *has* been blocked?" the French agent asked. "That was four years ago, you say..."

"The way in will still be there. The passage may be blocked, but you still have your plastique."

"I do," she agreed.

"And I *do* know another way in. But it's risky."

Stacey eyeballed him. "And this *isn't?*"

"That can wait. We need to suit up."

A half-hour later they reconvened in the Sands' suite, the trio entirely in black. The women wore insulated catsuits with holsters high on hips with untucked blouses tugged over their pistol butts. Everyone had a combat knife in their right boot. All wore black gloves and black stocking caps. Sand had on insulated black slacks and a thick black turtleneck; he apologized to the ladies for not having bullet-resistant vests for them as he put his on. He threw a black suit coat over his shoulder rig—as usual, Beretta in ankle holster, switchblade in pocket.

Walking to Tiergarten Park took only about five minutes from the Savoy via *Kantstraße*, which turned into *Budapester Strasse* just past the large Kaiser Wilhelm

Memorial Church. As before, they chased their breath. A biting wind hit them in the face, seemingly indifferent to which direction they went.

Turning north at *Hofjägerallee*, the trio followed it to the *Siegessäule*, the Victory Column erected in 1864 to celebrate the Prussians defeating the Danish army. From there, they cut east on the sidewalk just south of *Bundesstraße 2*, the sounds of light traffic carrying on the frigid air. They walked briskly to the *Bezirksamt Mitte*, a five-story government glass-and-concrete office building near where Sand had exited Hitler's tunnels four years ago.

Beyond the government office, on the little-traveled-at-night street behind the building, a manhole waited. Looking around, making sure no one was nearby, Sand pried the lid off and set it to one side.

Whispering, he said, "They could be anywhere between here and Brandenburg Gate, so tread softly and stay sharp. Silent running, ladies. Gestures only."

Wincing as she assessed the small opening, Charlotte said, "I do not think they bring the bomb in this way."

He shook his head. "No, they have access to doors big enough to allow trucks to enter with supplies. That's my other way in. But I don't know exactly where any of those doors are, and anyway they might be guarded, plus we don't have time to find one. That, however, is our other alternative."

"Always nice," Stacey said with a smirk, "to have options."

"As it is," Sand continued, "we barely have time to go in this way, find the bomb, deal with whoever comes at us with whatever they come at us with and...save the world."

"I am glad you put it that way," Charlotte said. "I would hate to think of it as saving Germans."

Former French freedom fighters, Sand knew, tended to hold a grudge.

He looked down into the black hole and the black hole looked back at him—no light, no sound. Wherever Kyla and her crew were, it wasn't right below, or even close by, which could be good or bad. Sand went down the ladder first into utter darkness, descending slowly and carefully.

When he reached the concrete floor, he pulled a penlight from his pocket and used it in both directions, seeing nothing either way, just the narrow beam it cast. No sounds, either, not even a drip of water or rustle of a rat. The cold down here matched above but without, at least, any wind to contend with.

He aimed the penlight up, turned it on, off, signaling Stacey to begin down the ladder.

He switched the light to his left hand and filled his right with the Walther, continuing to check both directions. As Stacey dropped to the floor, Sand shone the light up again, on, off, and Charlotte came down.

He had instructed her to leave the manhole cover to one side; they would risk someone noticing the lid and replacing it or seeing it as suspicious—little likelihood of either in the middle of the night. Better to keep their exit route clear.

Soon all three stood in the darkness with pistols drawn, as frozen as if the cold were even colder—still no sound, still no light. Sand shone the penlight down at the cement floor, which was dirty, some detritus but nothing major, fairly clear as far ahead as could be seen. He shone the light up—rusted girders. Few humans had been in this portion of the tunnels since the end of World War II. Those who exited back then had left in a hurry, this corridor wide enough to accommodate a car or even a small truck, though nothing indicated any vehicles had passed through here since the war.

This area smelled musty, different than the petrol-scented section where he had been held prisoner four years ago. While there would be rooms down here, Hitler's private air raid shelter-cum-apartment, the section Sand had been in was more like a low-ceilinged warehouse. He would be taking his little team in that direction.

With the penlight on, he indicated the way with a nod. The two women nodded back. His left shoulder almost brushed the wall and the women followed suit in a row close behind. Soon he switched off the light.

They worked their way along in pitch darkness, close to the wall but not touching it, the slight shuffling of their shoes on the dirty floor and their shallow, rapid breathing the only sounds. But he knew right where he was headed. He was betting Kyla would plant the bomb under the east end of Tiergarten Park, with the Brandenburg Gate, immediately across the *Ebertstraße*.

When they got to an intersecting tunnel, he reached his left hand back and touched Stacey. She stood in place, extended her hand back similarly to alert Charlotte. With the group paused, each with a shoulder pressed against the southern wall of the eastbound tunnel, Sand looked north—no sign of light. And still no sounds. Dropping to a knee, he stuck his head around the corner and looked south. Again, no light, no sound.

They crossed the intersecting tunnel single-file, and continued east in the same fashion, a shoulder near the wall, Sand in the lead, their progress painstakingly slow, the underground air ever chill. At least they couldn't see their breath—not enough light for it to register.

Finally, after a walk in the dark for nearly a kilometer,

Sand again alerted Stacey by reaching back to her, and she did the same with Charlotte. Again all three paused.

And now, finally, far-away, faintly echoing voices came to them. A distant motor started up, and Sand recognized it as a forklift. He smiled to himself.

They were getting close now.

They crept forward, crossing one intersecting corridor and, before long, another, each time requiring care and stealth that slowed their progress. But now they could now see a soft yellow glow ahead. The grunting of the forklift's motor was much louder now, but nonetheless they could make out a familiar female voice shrieking, "*Beeil dich, wir haben nicht viel Zeit!*"

Hurry up, we don't have much time!

Kyla Fluss.

Part of him liked how frazzled she sounded, how rattled. But that meant she knew they were on to her and worried they might be closing in, which of course they were. So she and her people would be on the alert.

The glow up ahead encouraged a certain night vision now. He made eye contact with Stacey and Charlotte behind him, holding up a "stop" palm. They waited for direction. Sand indicated he'd go forward for a look and come back. Another nod from each, then Charlotte guided Stacey down to a knee, and they hugged the wall—being seen was becoming a risk.

That applied to Sand as well.

He dropped to his belly, leopard-crawled along the wall in what was now only near-darkness, Walther at the ready. He stopped five meters short of where this corridor crossed another; in that intersection, Kyla's men were working, the forklift growling, its forks raised up into the back of a flatbed, canvas-framed truck. Work lights on poles on either side pointed their beams at the truck bed, a womb giving birth to a hellish child.

The forklift driver was a big man with a stocking cap and a gray overcoat, a Schmeisser MP40 on a sling under his right arm so as not to impede his driving. The driver backed the forklift up, revealing a pallet atop its forks bearing a huge gray spiky metal ball. The forklift's exhaust told Sand how hard a time the vehicle was having with the weight of the bomb.

He counted eight men around the back of the truck, Kyla standing on the far side, yelling orders in German. She wore a black leather trench coat thrown open over a red silk blouse and gray jodhpurs with black-leather boots, her hands on her hips like Rommel berating his men, which was what she was doing, her mane of blonde hair wild and loose.

Sand had mounted this raid entertaining the notion of letting Kyla Fluss live. Not out of mercy or feelings generated by their brief fling, rather out of wanting to preserve what she knew about the renewal of the Reich. Pity for that to die with her.

Hanging off the black belt of her jodhpurs was a remote control, the kind the fancier televisions had. While the bomb would almost certainly operate off a timer—designed to allow Kyla to make her escape well before the bomb exploded—that remote control indicated a backup. Should the planting of the bomb be interrupted, that clicker allowed for detonation even if Kyla's demented effort became a suicide mission.

The crew Kyla had assembled looked more like workmen than killers—thugs after a paycheck not Nazis with a cause. Their togs ran more toward sailor or construction worker, not the tailored SS stormtroopers who once haunted these cement catacombs—pea coats, gloves, stocking caps. Had their wardrobe ended there, Sand might have taken care to spare their lives. But they all also carried Schmeisser submachine guns, a decision that sealed their fate.

He watched as the forklift slowly lowered the bomb-on-its-pallet. With the load only inches off the floor, the vehicle slowly turned, lumbering away from Sand, down the tunnel to the east...

...heading for a spot near the Brandenburg Gate, no doubt.

Kyla walked along next to the vehicle, guiding it and its driver, like a mother whose baby was taking its first steps. Two machine-gun-carrying workmen swiveled the lights-on-stands to better illuminate the tunnel.

Six of the eight men followed along behind the bomb, sauntering as if headed toward their neighborhood *rathskeller*, possibly unaware they might be firing the opening shot—and what a shot—of a third World War.

Sand was about to rush the remaining two thugs, intending to take them out silently, when a plume of mist from an exhalation of breath announced someone not in sight.

At least three men, then—damn it.

"*Wer hat eine Zigarette?*" said the unseen third man.

The one nearest Sand replied in German, "That's an atomic bomb—should you be smoking so close to it?"

So some of these "workmen" were Nazis, Sand thought. *Or very short-sighted mercenaries.*

The third man stepped into Sand's line of sight—burly with shabby clothes. "The bomb is leaving, I'm staying. Do you have a *Scheiß* cigarette or not?"

The one with his back to Sand pulled a pack from an inside pocket, shook out a cigarette.

"And a light?"

The man lit the burly man's cigarette.

The three stood watching the forklift disappear down the tunnel. Sand gestured for Charlotte and Stacy to join him and they did. He assigned a target for each. He would take the burly man. They all knew that if they made any noise, they would be initiating a firefight in which they were both outnumbered and outgunned.

They moved forward silently, knives out. Sand was ready to grab the burly man from behind when his target's attention was drawn to the motion of Charlotte slitting the throat of hers. The burly man was about to yell when Sand clasped his left hand over the open mouth and swung his right hand around and sank the switchblade into the man's heart. He and the burly man did a sad little dance that started out a samba and eased into a tango before the music stopped and Sand eased his partner to the cement, where the two dead targets Charlotte and Stacey had made already lay in bloody pools.

For all that, they hadn't generated a lot of noise, but hadn't exactly been silent either. Charlotte snatched up a Schmeisser, pulled Stacey—a little dazed, having for the first time cut a throat—behind the truck with her. Sand collected the other two Schmeissers and presented one to Stacey. His eyes asked his wife if she was all right and her nod said she was.

Then the three waited, listened.

Finally they heard footfalls, echoing, unhurried, the other six workmen coming back casually—just another day at the work site, unloading an atom bomb. Sand sprinted from behind the truck to the other side of the intersecting tunnel.

"*Ey!*" someone yelled.

Gunfire spattered the walls and floor around him, but

as the first two gunmen lurched into the light, Sand and Charlotte blasted them from either side. Both gunmen staggered, stumbled, fell, dead ragged things. Sand and Charlotte blistered the tunnel, emptying their magazines, Stacey ready but not joining in, the other woman in better position. The air filled with the aroma of cordite.

When their clips were empty, Sand and Charlotte tossed the Schmeissers and pulled their pistols, the trio falling back into listening mode. All they heard was the moan of a wounded man.

Sand crawled out and grabbed a work light on its pole and pulled it to the full length of its cord, sending its beam down the tunnel. No one shot back at them, which didn't necessarily mean that only the moaning man was still alive among the fallen enemy.

The work light revealed four men on the cement, one writhing, his legs a bloody mess—the moaning man. The other three appeared dead. Slowly, Sand moved forward, Charlotte and Stacey hanging back. The women had switched positions, Stacey now leaning out past the rear of the truck, Schmeisser in her hands.

With the exception of the moaning man, these were obvious corpses. Down in the darkness, the forklift kept chugging. Kyla wasn't going to let a little firefight stop her.

Schmeisser fire erupted behind him and Sand swung with his weapon ready to respond; but it was Stacey, popped out from behind the truck to stitch the moaning man's body with machine-gun fire—he had stopped moaning long enough to drag his bloody legs and crawl toward the Schmeisser he'd dropped getting shot.

Sand exchanged glances with his wife—his sad shrug said, *Brave, but what did it get him?* Her pragmatic shrug said, *Put out of his misery.*

Stacey and Charlotte fell in behind Sand, Stacey giving Charlotte the Schmeisser now, then getting out her Walther. Sand trotted down the tunnel, and the women kept up; but soon the light from the spotlight gave way to shadow, and then darkness.

He and his little party slowed. They could still hear the forklift, and could see it down the tunnel, barely, a flashlight bobbing next to it, an odd strobing effect.

The trio kept a steady pace. Up ahead, the forklift—guided only by Kyla's electric torch—moved slowly ahead. Sand didn't dare switch on the penlight and give Kyla a target, and to move faster could mean walking into a trap. The forklift's growl was a steady thing, the vehicle apparently not encountering any surprises, no ancient garbage blocking the path for example. So Sand's little army would go straight down the middle, too.

Then the forklift groaned to a stop.

The invading trio picked up their pace, building to a run, and then the forklift came out of the darkness like a beast leaping from a cave; but this beast sat, fully stopped. The bomb was no longer on the forklift, sitting on its pallet on the cement like a slightly undersize wrecking ball with a spiky surface. Kyla was appraising her handiwork with a smile, her pale face and blonde hair floating in darkness that swallowed her black leather and gray jodhpurs and gave up flashes of her silk scarlet blouse.

The stocking-capped driver in the gray overcoat shut off the vehicle and was sliding out of the right side of it, lugging a Schmeisser. Sand had not been close enough to recognize him before, but now he did: this was Rocky Rivers, the "husband" of Kyla Fluss.

With the forklift's engine off, their running in that echoey tunnel announced them, prompting Rivers to spin around, raising his Schmeisser.

Charlotte punched holes in his chest with two shots and, even as Rivers hit the cement, the invading trio did the same, only they were still alive, while at the same time Kyla returned fire with two shots of her own. Then her flashlight winked off, leaving them in utter darkness again, their night vision struggling to adjust.

Sand shouted, "*Tell me where he is, Kyla, and you don't have to die down here!*"

"*Where* who *is, John?*" came a voice from the darkness. Casual. Insane.

"*Your father. Von Koerber, he's calling himself now. Until he reveals himself to the world.*"

Kyla's laughter echoed. "*My father died in 1945 in this bunker! Ask anyone!*"

"*And this great new plot is all* your *doing?*"

"*Mine and Milan's...the man that you killed! My* real *husband. And the reason why I don't care if I die down here, too—because* you *killed the love of my life!*"

He knew what she would do next—use that TV remote clicker on her belt. He had no choice—he walked toward her. "Let's finish it now, Kyla! But we'll always have Berlin..."

Eyes wild and wide, Kyla aimed her flashlight at him then shrieked with laughter as she shot him in the chest.

Sand fell to the tunnel floor, giving Stacey a clear sight line to Kyla and her flashlight. His wife fired once. Astounded by her mortality, Kyla dropped her pistol and flashlight as she toppled forward, the flashlight rolling in a lazy circle, the beam coming to a stop on her lifeless blue eyes, the black-edged hole in her forehead oozing a single scarlet teardrop.

Stacey helped Sand up. "Are you insane? She could've

been a head-shot fanatic like you!"

"*She* was insane *and* a fanatic," Sand said, wincing after the impact of Kyla's round, "which is why I had to risk it. I had to make sure she didn't use that remote control or we'd all be dead."

Charlotte, on the other side of him now, said, "All of us and much of the rest of Berlin. By the way, do either of you know how to defuse an atomic bomb?"

Ignoring the pain, Sand went over to the dead woman and plucked the remote control from her belt. He removed the batteries, scattered them to the cement, and said, "That's a start."

Stacey, having followed her husband to Kyla's corpse, picked up the woman's flashlight and went to the bomb on the pallet. She ran the beam across the spiny surface until she found a hatch that revealed a digital read-out, seconds counting down in white against black.

Sand and Charlotte came over and had a look.

Charlotte said, "Just as you suspected, John—it's set for December 11 at 12:00:01 AM."

"We'll never know for sure," Sand said, "but she might have been preparing to re-set the timer to get herself far enough away to feel safe."

"Time to call Double M?" Charlotte asked.

They were speaking so softly, their words didn't echo.

Sand said, "Time to call Double M."

CHAPTER SIXTEEN
BOMB'S AWAY

—

Back home in Houston, Stacey Sand was experiencing the fourth case of butterflies of her lifetime.

Just days ago, Stacey, John and Charlotte—in the same truck Kyla's crew used to bring the bomb to the *Führerbunker*—had conveyed the still-armed device to an empty warehouse beyond the outskirts of Berlin, getting the deadly thing away from the divided city's center until a GUILE-supervised bomb squad could take over. Riding around the bumpy streets of Berlin with an atomic bomb in the back of a World War Two-vintage truck had been nerve-wracking enough, and yet still not butterfly inducing.

Nor had the fluttering creatures attacked her when the three agents returned to Las Vegas for debriefing by Lord Marbury himself, who actually seemed pleased to see them. Double M reported a round-up of Nazi collaborators in Berlin ("Not your *Texas* style of round-up, Mrs. Sand," Double M had added wryly). Also (he let them know), in the scorched ruins of Inalco House, an otherwise unrecognizable corpse had been identified, through dental records, as Victor Von Koerber.

"That may be good enough for *you*, sir," Sand said, "but not me."

Double M, uncharacteristically shrugging off that near insubordination, said, "We are continuing to investigate Von Koerber, despite Argentine authorities deeming him dead—they are not, after all, the most reliable source when it comes to dead Nazis. And we are monitoring any activities that might indicate the would-be return of the Reich may still be in the works. I pledge to you, Triple Seven, that you will be kept in the loop every step of the way."

"I will hold you to that, sir."

The three GUILE agents shared a friendly dinner at the Bootlegger Bistro, a cozy Italian place. They chatted about everything except the experiences they'd shared of late, and laughed and had too much red wine, winding up toasting the late Jaime. Stacey felt ashamed to have doubted the woman, feeling surprising warmth for Charlotte, possibly her only real competition for John Sand's heart on the planet.

And still no butterflies caused by that situation, either.

Now, however, the damned things were very much fluttering in her stomach, tiny wings beating against the lining. All because she had to summon the courage to talk to John about whatever it was he'd been brooding about since they returned this evening to *Plata Luna*.

She had slipped into a black negligee that always put that certain look in his eye, making sure her hair and makeup were perfect in their lightly applied fashion; then she slipped a black silk robe over the nightie and saw a knockout looking back at her from the bedroom mirror.

But her feeling of confidence vanished and that flutter found its way into her tummy again as she entered the living room. Her husband, in black lounging pajamas, was seated on the end of the brown leather couch, feet on an ottoman; flames snapped in the fieldstone fireplace over which their own portrait—commissioned for a small fortune from Norman Rockwell—looked contentedly down. John was looking neither at the fire nor themselves in oil (fittingly), but out the picture window to his left into a Texas night that was clear and star-flung and yet so very dark.

"Talk to me, John," she said, settling next to him, tucking her legs up under her. "You're not having *doubts* again, about this crazy life we're leading...?"

He turned to her quickly, obviously not noticing her presence till she'd spoken.

"Certainly not," he said with a smile that took work. "You make almost as good a field agent as you do a wife."

"Then, darling...what is it?"

His eyes returned to the window on the night. "He's out there. I can feel him. The madman is out there."

"You heard what Lord Marbury said." She touched his arm. "Von Koerber is dead, and that means—"

"Possibly nothing. Possibly anything. The Global Unit remains on the alert." He shrugged dismissively, almost contemptuously.

Stacey leaned closer. "And Double M promised you'd be the first to know, if anything turns up. John, we both heard that terrible woman say she didn't care if she died 'down here too'—like her father."

"Kyla may merely have meant the others who died that night at our hands, like Rivers. I'm telling you, her father is alive."

She threw up a hand. "All right. He's alive. But if so, he's in hiding. You've broken his network, ruined his plans. If he knows what's good for him, he's going to stay hidden. And if he does poke his evil head out again—"

"I'll kill him."

"And if you need me, I'll help you do it. I'll reload your gun, I'll drill his bodyguards, I'll hold your coat while you strangle him."

That made him smile and this time he didn't have to work at it.

"He killed my friend," John said with a chilling calm. "The world mourned a great man, and that's as it should be. America can write it off as some lone-nut gunman. But I won't have my friends murdered out from under me. I simply won't bloody have it."

She nodded. "I understand. And I love you for your loyalty and your bravery, but you can't let this consume you. Consume *us.* We have lives to live. And perhaps one day...a family."

He held her hand. "Perhaps."

She squeezed his. "But for now, we'll keep your...quest for justice, for vengeance...to ourselves. Go around saying you think Hitler is still alive and you plan to do something about it, and, well...you'll only get us in the *National Enquirer* next to UFOs and Liz and Dick."

That actually made him laugh a little.

With his usual impeccable timing, Cuchillo entered in full butler livery, including white gloves for a change, in a puckish display of respect. He had a bottle of champagne chilling in a bucket of ice and two flutes. He poured John a small amount, gave it to him.

"Does this meet with your approval, sir?"

"1937 Bollinger? An excellent vintage. Yes, Cuchillo, this will do nicely."

The major domo poured for them both.

"If there's nothing else," the ex-*federale* said, "I'll be

retiring for the evening."

"That's fine, Cuchillo," John said. "Thank you. Dispatch any intruders with prejudice."

"As always," Cuchillo said with a nod and a faint smile.

Alone, Sand said to her, "What shall we drink to?"

She said, "How about...to Camelot?"

Clinking glasses with her, John said, "To Camelot."

* * * * * *

John Sand knew the Arthurian legend well, and the Broadway show that had drawn upon it, which President Kennedy had taken so to heart.

But the final curtain could not come down as long as Mordred, the king's evil rival, was still out there, waiting to be found.

AN ANNOTATION FOR THE FILES OF JOHN SAND

———

Thanks to retired Detective Lieutenant Chris Kauffman, our resident Gil Grissom, for his knowledge of weapons and their varied uses.

Thanks also to Jim O'Connell, our resident Bill Nye The Science Guy, for information on Uranium 235.

You both made time travel back to the swingin' Sixties easier for us, if not for our protagonists. Neither of you is responsible for our mistakes, crimes we are quite capable of committing unaided and unabetted.

Thank you to Barb Collins and Pam Clemens, and our agent Dominic Abel.

And thanks, of course, to editor Paul Bishop and publisher Mike Bray and everyone at Wolfpack.

ABOUT THE AUTHORS

———

MAX ALLAN COLLINS was named a Grand Master in 2017 by the Mystery Writers of America. He is a three-time winner of the Private Eye Writers of America "Shamus" award, receiving the PWA "Eye" for Life Achievement (2006) and their "Hammer" award for making a major contribution to the private eye genre with the Nathan Heller saga (2012).

His graphic novel *Road to Perdition* (1998) became the Academy Award-winning Tom Hanks film, followed by prose sequels and several graphic novels. His other comics credits include the syndicated strip "Dick Tracy"; "Batman"; and his own "Ms. Tree" and "Wild Dog."

His innovative Quarry novels were adapted as a 2016 TV series by Cinemax. His other suspense series include Eliot Ness, Krista Larson, Reeder and Rogers, and the "Disaster" mysteries. He has completed twelve "Mike Hammer" novels begun by the late Mickey Spillane; his audio novel, *Mike Hammer: The Little Death* with Stacy Keach, won a 2011 Audie for Best Original Work.

For five years, he was the licensing writer for TV's

*CSI: Crime Scene Investigation (*and its spin-offs*)*, writing best-selling novels, graphic novels, and video games. His tie-in books have appeared on the USA TODAY and *New York Times* bestseller lists, including *Saving Private Ryan, Air Force One,* and *American Gangster.*

Collins has written and directed four features and two documentaries, including the Lifetime movie *Mommy* (1996) and *Mike Hammer's Mickey Spillane* (1998) featured on the Criterion edition of *Kiss Me Deadly*; he scripted *The Expert,* a 1995 HBO World Premiere and the film festival favorite *The Last Lullaby* (2009) from his novel *The Last Quarry.* His Edgar-nominated play *Eliot Ness: An Untouchable Life* (2004) became a PBS special, and he has co-authored (with A. Brad Schwartz) two non-fiction books on Ness, *Scarface and the Untouchable* (2018) and *Eliot Ness and the Mad Butcher* (2020).

Collins and his wife, writer Barbara Collins, live in Iowa; as "Barbara Allan," they have collaborated on sixteen novels, including the "Trash 'n' Treasures" mysteries, *Antiques Flee Market* winning the *Romantic Times* Best Humorous Mystery Novel award of 2009. Their son Nathan has translated numerous novels into English from Japanese, as well as video games and manga.

MATTHEW V. CLEMENS is a writer and teacher whose first book was a non-fiction true-crime title, *Dead Water: the Klindt Affair* (1995, with Pat Gipple). He has co-written numerous books with Max Allan Collins, the pair having collaborated on over thirty novels and numerous short stories, as well as the much-lauded non-fiction work, *The History of Mystery* (2001). They also contributed an essay to the Edgar-nominated *In Pursuit of Spenser* (2012).

In addition the duo has produced several comic books,

four graphic novels, a computer game, and over a dozen mystery jigsaw puzzles for such famous TV properties as *CSI* (and its spin-offs), *NCIS, Buffy the Vampire Slayer, Hellboy,* and *The Mentalist,* as well as tie-in novels for *Bones, Dark Angel* and *Criminal Minds.* A number of the team's books made the USA TODAY bestseller list.

Matt also worked with Max on the bestselling "Reeder and Rogers" debut thriller, *Supreme Justice* (2014), and shared byline on its two sequels, *Fate of the Union* (2015) and *Executive Order* (2017). Their short stories have been collected by Wolfpack in the anthology, *Murderlized.* Matt has also published a number of solo short stories and worked on numerous book projects with other authors, both non-fiction and fiction, including R. Karl Largent on several of the late author's bestselling techno-thrillers. He has also worked as a book doctor for numerous other writers.

Matt lives in Davenport, Iowa with his wife, Pam, a retired teacher.

A LOOK AT: MURDERLIZED: STORIES
BY MAX ALLAN COLLINS AND MATTHEW V. CLEMENS

A COLLECTION OF EXCITING, SUSPENSEFUL TALES.

The title story, Murderlized, finds Moe Howard of The Three Stooges playing amateur private eye in Hollywood of 1937, solving the murder of the man the comedy team "stooged" for, Ted Healy.

Moe isn't the only unlikely detective in the short story collection, as famed writer Damon Runyon seeks The Devil's Face and a young female detective and her rough-and-tumble partner are Out for Blood.

Max Allan Collins and Matthew V. Clemens, whose collaborations include the bestselling CSI novels and the Reeder and Rogers series (Supreme Justice), collect eleven of their sometimes sexy, often violent, always exciting short stories, which range from police procedure to chilling horror, including the short story Lie Beside Me that was the first appearance of John Sand, star of Come Spy with Me.

AVAILABLE NOW